"Hey!" Cassandra was excited, even if Samantha wasn't. "You're *psychic,* amiga! This is just so neat! Do something clever."

"Negative," Dr. Reese pronounced over Ashley's readings. "Right, Cassandra, let's have you."

Grinning, Cassandra hurried over, taking Ashley's place in the chair. It was still warm. She rested her hands on the arms while the two students stuck the wires to her head. They felt a bit clammy, but not unbearably so.

"Right," the guy said. "Try to blank your mind. That's probably not hard."

That annoyed her a little. What did he think she was? A bimbo? But she played along, trying not to think about anything.

There was a slight tingle in her skin around the wires. And then the universe exploded.

The Outer Limits™

A whole new dimension in
adventure . . .

#1 The Zanti Misfits
#2 The Choice
#3 The Time Shifter
#4 The Lost
#5 The Invaders
#6 The Innocent
#7 The Vanished

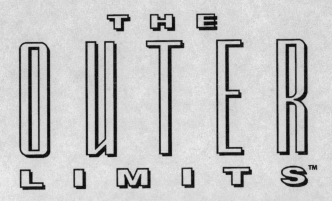

THE OUTER LIMITS™

THE NIGHTMARE

JOHN PEEL

A TOM DOHERTY ASSOCIATES BOOK
NEW YORK

This is a work of fiction. All the characters and events portrayed in this book are either products of the author's imagination or are used fictitiously.

THE OUTER LIMITS #8: THE NIGHTMARE

™ and © 1998 Metro-Goldwyn-Mayer Studios Inc. All rights reserved.
The Outer Limits is a trademark of Metro-Goldwyn-Mayer Studios Inc., and is licensed by MGM Consumer Products.

A Tor Book
Published by Tom Doherty Associates, Inc.
175 Fifth Avenue
New York, NY 10010

Tor® is a registered trademark of Tom Doherty Associates, Inc.

ISBN: 0-812-57565-2

First edition: December 1998

Printed in the United States of America

0 9 8 7 6 5 4 3 2 1

For Zoltan Takacs

We all have dreams—sometimes pleasurable, sometimes terrifying. Many make no sense at all, and some, at the time, seem to be perfectly sensible. Some dreams are embarrassing, some exciting. Many are simply disjointed.

Some people claim that dreams break down the barriers of our minds, freeing them to roam into the past and future. There are cases of people dreaming about things yet to come.

But nobody quite knows exactly what dreams are, or what causes them. Are they messages from our subconscious minds? The brain sifting through experiences of the day? Unconnected images flitting like butterflies across our sleeping thoughts? Or could it just be that they are the result of our minds attempting to make sense of something much greater and more mysterious than we can ever know?

CHAPTER 1

MUSTN'T STOP . . . MUST *NOT sleep!!*
Desolation.

She stared all around herself, shuddering at what she saw. Once, she knew, there had been houses and gardens, where trees and flowers exploded with color and scent. Now, vaguely smoking, there were only ruins—portions of houses sticking out of mud and dust like the bones of an ancient dinosaur being uncovered. The ground smoked slightly, and the only scent now was the stench of sulphur and burning.

The sky was midnight-dark, but she didn't have a clue what time it was. For all she knew, it could be midday. Tightly woven clouds obscured the sun—if there was one—muttering ominously to themselves. It was on the verge of a torrential downpour, but it never tipped over into actual activity. Only the grumble of thunder and the halfhearted flicker of stillborn lightning—no rain, though the air was charged with it.

What was happening? She knew somehow that this wasn't how things were supposed to be. This wasn't normal. Life wasn't like this! But the memories that she needed, she couldn't touch. They danced outside her grasp, leaving her confused and unsure of herself.

How long had this been going on? She felt as though she had only moments ago awakened from some terrible dream—only to discover that reality was even worse. But that wasn't possible. She was standing in the middle of a shattered town, and she had to have been doing *something* just moments ago. But she couldn't remember what.

There was a fog and a lack of color in her mind, just as there was on the face of the ground. The soil was dead, nothing growing in it, and in the poor light simply shades of black and gray. Her mind felt the same way: frozen, unfocused, confused. Her memories had fled, and were staying out of reach of her numb thoughts. She couldn't remember who she was, where she was, or why she was here.

There was something in there that seemed urgent, but she couldn't quite get ahold of it. It was slipping out of her mental fingers each time she tried to grasp and examine it. There was something . . . but it wouldn't come to light.

Something to do with people . . . and hunting . . . She looked around in sudden alarm, but there was nothing moving, save for wisps of smoke.

A dream ... Was *this* a dream? She looked around, and shivered. It *ought* to be a dream. Surely no place as sterile and desolate as this should exist in the world. Wasn't the world a place of growing things, of flying, singing birds, of cheeky squirrels, contented cats and barking dogs? Wasn't it where people laughed, and played, and loved, and did things with fierce intensity and passion? It surely couldn't be a grim and bleak place like this!

So, was she dreaming?

She didn't know. How could she tell? Maybe it was a dream, and nothing more than that. Her mind was so numb, she didn't know. But wasn't there something you could do to find out if you were dreaming? Oh, yes ... pinch yourself. That was it.

She looked at her nails. All broken, uneven, disgusting. No polish, no buffing. They looked as if she'd been digging in the earth with her hands. She shrugged. For all she knew, she had been. Steeling herself, she grabbed a patch of skin on her bare arm and dug her nails in.

Dimly she was aware that this hurt her. She looked at the angry patch of skin, and saw she'd drawn blood. It trickled over her nails as she watched, disconnected. It *did* hurt, but it was such a small pain in everything else that she felt that it hardly registered. Weird.

So she *wasn't* dreaming. Then why couldn't she remember where she was, who she was, why she was here—and why everything seemed to be so wrong?

Her body felt as if it were dragging her down. She felt like a zombie, her limbs heavy weights, her mind nonfunctioning. Her thoughts were clouded, and it was so difficult to concentrate. But she knew that she *had* to focus, even if she couldn't bring herself to do it. There was something important that she should be aware of.

Something to do with the people. But *where* were the people? And why was she so frightened?

Glancing around, her head hurt. There was no real change in the environment, no matter which way she looked. There were different arrangements of shattered homes, barely more than sticks or bricks or parts of a wall here and there. She rather thought she could see, half submerged in mud, the burned-out wreckage of a car. There was the stump of a streetlamp, wires tangled, and a few shattered trees, skeletal fingers of death. But it was all the same sort of wreckage all around her.

There were no signs of life but herself. Well, if it was night, everyone might be sleeping, of course. Or they could all be sheltering from the impending rain. But she didn't think so. She was vaguely sure that there wasn't much of anything left alive. But she didn't know how she knew that, or even if it was accurate.

So the only thing for her to look at was herself. Okay, then, look at herself. She'd already checked out her filthy nails. What else? She stared at her bare arms, and saw that the blood had started to clot. There were other cuts on her arms. Had she done that to herself? She couldn't remember. Slowly, she moved her attention to the rest of her body. She was wearing a T-shirt that might once have been yellow, but she couldn't be sure. It was ripped in several places, and she was aware that under each spot there was a welt or cut on her body. She had no idea what had caused them, though. The pain from them was part of that dull background agony, but only a part of it. There was a wristwatch on her left wrist, but the thing was broken and dead. Fumbling, she pulled it off and let it drop into the mud.

She was wearing blue jeans. These, like the T-shirt, were scuffed and torn, and not for the sake of fashion, either. She looked as if she'd been attacked or something.

Attacked . . .

She *almost* had it, but it had flittered away again! But that thought had seemed to be close to home, somehow. *Attacked* . . . Well, that would explain her cuts, and her general feeling of absolute tiredness. And maybe the memory loss, too. Had she been hit over the head, and was she suffering from concussion?

She felt her head, fingering the skin under a thick tangle of hair that hadn't been combed. There was no sign of a bump, or cut, or even anywhere more sensitive than anywhere else. Her fingers caught in a knot of hair, and she pulled it around to look at it. Stringy, dirty, unwashed, and unbrushed—for how long? It was hard even to make out the color, except to know that it was dark. Well, whoever she was, she wasn't a blond. Maybe that was a start.

Okay, back to taking inventory. She stared at her feet and was surprised to discover that they were bare. No shoes? That didn't seem to be right. She was sure normal people were supposed to wear shoes, or sandals, or sneakers. Not to wallow in the mud with naked toes. So what had happened to her shoes? Once again, she didn't have a clue.

She reached into her pockets, but there was nothing at all in any of them. No jewelry, no necklace, nothing. All she had was her clothes, and there weren't too many of those. No ID, no purse or money. Nothing that normal people tended to carry—unless they'd fallen somewhere? She glanced all around, but there was nothing to be seen—unless you counted mud.

Well, she was getting nowhere just about as fast as anyone ever could.

There wasn't really any point in staying where she was. The air was kind of chilly, raising goose bumps on her exposed arms. She shivered. Maybe it was just this area that was like this. Perhaps over the next rise there would be houses, warmth, clothing . . .

People.

That thought made her shudder, too. Didn't she want to see other people? She had a vague memory of being in a crowded, happy place, with lots of people and laughter and noise. How had she come to this wilderness from there? And where had all of the people gone?

Attack . . . people . . .

There was a connection. Somehow she knew that. People couldn't be trusted. They would tell you that you were their friend, but they were lying. As soon as they could, they'd attack you.

She stopped, startled. Was that what had happened to her? Someone had betrayed her and attacked her? She just didn't know.

With a shrug, she started walking. Since the direction didn't seem to matter, she simply started off in the direction she was facing, one step after another. Her whole body ached. Her bones were weary, her muscles tired, her head heavy, her brain fried. One step, another. Squelch, squelch . . .

And nothing changed. There was mud or there was dust. There was the threat of rain that never became real. There was a smell of decay, but nothing she could see that was causing it. Her stomach felt tight, her lips parched. How long was it since she'd last eaten or drunk anything? Why was she constantly asking herself these questions when she didn't have a clue as to any of the answers?

Then she stopped, startled. It was a *feeling*, in the back of her mind. Somehow, she knew it was real. A shivering in her soul, a touch of icy evil.

People were coming . . .

She didn't know how she knew, but she was sure she was right. And they mustn't see her! If they did, they would . . . they would . . .

What? She didn't know. But she also knew that she didn't *want* to know. And she most definitely didn't want to be found out. She had to hide.

Hide! That was a joke! There wasn't anywhere to hide. Just mud and broken fingers of ruined houses.

Wearily, she headed for the closest one. At least she wasn't leaving a trail; the mud simply smoothed out after she'd plodded through it. Drawing closer to the wrecked home, she saw that it was little more than a few tiny sections of wall. She winced, but she knew that *they* were closer now, and she had no other options. Well, she could hardly get any filthier or more uncomfortable. She collapsed beside the wall fragment, staying low to the ground. If she were lucky, it would hide her. She was facedown in the mud, her frightened eyes scanning the gloom for any sign of movement.

There! To the north! She could make out six or seven people, all staggering through the night. They were all dressed as poorly as she was. But all of them carried weapons of one kind or another. One man had a rifle, held at the ready. A woman beside him carried a butcher's knife. A couple of others had sticks, either from branches or the broken legs of chairs or tables. One had what looked like a bicycle chain.

They were hunting for her . . .

She *knew* that was true. That was why she was so scared and tired and filthy. These people hated her for some reason, and were hunting for her. They wanted to kill her. They wanted to break her bones, hear her scream, drain her blood drop by drop and make her die in slow, agonizing stages.

But she didn't know *why*. What had she done that they should hate her so? These people surely couldn't all be killers. Why, then, did they want to hurt her so much?

She watched as the group staggered through the night. Two of them had flashlights and were scanning the ground as they plodded on. But they didn't come anywhere near where she lay facedown in the mud, terrified of being found. After a few minutes, they passed on. But she knew they would be back. And she knew that there were others like them, also hunting for her.

What could she do? Was there anywhere safe for her, where she could rest, and clean up, and eat and drink? Was there anywhere where she could *sleep*? She could feel an overwhelming tiredness in herself, right down to her soul. She wanted to close her eyes, and sleep forever. But that would be dangerous. The searchers would find her, and then they would kill her.

And, besides, there were worse things waiting when she slept. Much, much worse. She discovered that the only thing that terrified her more than staying awake was going to sleep . . .

What could she do?

She wished she had tears left to cry, but they were all gone. They had been used up long ago. All she had left was bleakness and despair. She didn't even have a name, or an identity, or a possession to call her own. Only despair inside, and desolation outside.

Staggering to her feet, she started shuffling along again. It didn't make any difference, really, where she went. Only that she keep moving. And only that she shouldn't sleep.

A moment later, she stopped, looking around herself, as if for the first time.

Where was she? Who was she? What was happening to her?

How long had this been going on?

CHAPTER 2

"I'M NOT SO sure about this, Cassie."

Cassandra Baker tossed her head and laughed. "Sammy," she replied, "you're *never* sure about things. Trust me. When have I ever steered you wrong?" She looked at her friend with all the innocence she could muster.

"What time frame?" Samantha Marlowe asked dryly. "Your whole life, or just the past week or so?"

"Don't be so negative," Cassandra answered. "This is going to be fun. Plus, you'll get to meet some eligible college boys. How can we lose?"

Samantha bit her lip nervously. The two girls were a study in opposites. Samantha was introverted, almost brooding, with a strong streak of pessimism in her that seemed out of place on this delightful spring day. Cassandra was a good six inches taller, and far more slender. She was vivacious and attractive and nothing seemed to bother her—certainly not any memories of messed-up plans from the long-dead past.

"It sounds so lame," Samantha finally said.

"*You* sound lame, Sammy," Cassandra commented. "Come on, be a devil. It'll be fun, we'll get some brownie points for doing it, and we'll meet guys. Aside from getting paid, how much better could it get?"

Samantha looked at the notice on the bulletin board again, obviously still with reservations. It was one of about twenty on the school board, and it was, naturally, the one that had caught Cassandra's eye.

VOLUNTEERS NEEDED FOR PSYCHIC EXPERIMENT

"I think it's dangerous to mess around with things you don't understand," Samantha said, as firmly as she could.

"Right," scoffed Cassandra. "As if you understand cell phones and televisions! You just take them on faith!"

"You know what I mean," her friend said stubbornly. "Messing about with psychic stuff can get you into deep doo-doo. Demons and things."

Cassandra shook her head. "Honestly, Sammy, you don't *believe* in that sort of garbage, do you? Anyway, it's not like they'll be using Ouija boards, or raising the dead. Or even dancing around a maypole. It's a *scientific* study, it says. It'll be doing dumb stuff like Rhine cards."

"What?"

Cassandra rolled her eyes. "Honestly, there are days when I think you don't know *anything* useful."

"Only my lessons," Samantha said dryly. "Which don't seem to be your top priority."

Ignoring the jibe, Cassandra explained. "They're a deck of cards with five symbols on them. One guy looks at them where the test subject—me, for example—can't see them. Then I have to try to pick up telepathically an image of whatever he's looking at. Then they score you on it. Pure chance is one in five right. If you get more than that, you're psychic."

"Or cheating," Samantha suggested. "It still sounds to me like you're opening your mind up to dark forces."

"Which century are you living in?" Cassandra asked. "Honestly, you'll be saying the Earth's flat, next. Come on, Sammy, let's do it."

Finally Samantha sighed. "It's against my better judgment," she muttered.

But Cassandra knew that this was just a last-ditch salvo, and she had already won the war. She hugged her friend. "That's the spirit!"

Samantha rolled her eyes. "You could have picked a better word."

Cassandra just laughed, and they headed for their lockers. Their school, Stollville Junior High, was the largest in the area, but that didn't make it huge. People from the surrounding towns were bussed in to make up the numbers, so it was generally noisy and crowded. Today was no exception. Both girls were greeted by friends of both sexes. Cassandra accepted this as simply the normal order of things. She and Samantha were popular—though Samantha more because she was half of the team rather than in her own right. But she and Samantha went back a long way since they only lived two doors apart. They'd been best friends since first grade, despite their frequent clashes on just about every subject. Cassandra always acted as if disagreements were unimportant, and Samantha always placed friendship over her gloom-and-doom attitude.

"Hi, gorgeous," Troy called out as they approached.

"And who are you referring to?" Cassandra asked, grinning. Troy was just a good friend—so far—since he was actually dating Ashley Curran. But she was sure that wouldn't last.

"Well, it's hard to pick," he answered, matching her grin. "Both of you have a good claim to the description."

"Flatterer," Cassandra answered, enjoying the attention. If only Samantha could get into the mood, she'd have a better time. Instead, she just raised a disbelieving eyebrow.

"Guilty," Troy agreed. "You guys see that announcement about the psychic thingy?"

"Cassie wants us to sign up," Samantha replied.

"I figured it was her kind of thing," Troy said, not surprised. "Ashley and I have already decided to go along, so why don't the four of us head over there after school?"

"You just want to be seen with the three prettiest girls in school," Cassandra accused him.

Troy threw up his hands. "Whoa! I can see there's

no fooling you! You *must* be psychic! They'll love you at this thing.''

Laughing, the three of them headed for class.

The psychic auditions—or whatever they were— were being held at the local Knights of Columbus Hall. It was used more for birthday parties or flower shows, and it seemed kind of odd to Cassandra. But, whatever—she could live with it. Cassandra liked Ashley, and could even *almost* forgive her for having snagged Troy before she could. The four of them were having a few laughs as they entered the hall. Just inside was a trestle table, and behind it a woman in her twenties. Grad student, most likely, since this was being run by the local university.

"Sign in, please," she said. "Name, address, phone number. Then sign the consent forms."

"Consent forms?" Samantha asked, immediately zeroing in on the most ominous object present. "Why do we need those?"

"*You* don't; we do," the woman replied. "They're standard for these sorts of tests."

Afraid that Samantha would back out and ruin the fun, Cassandra sighed. "Look, they just want to cover themselves in case, okay? It's no big deal." She signed hers with a flourish.

"Protect themselves from *what*?" Samantha demanded.

"Lawsuits brought by pessimistic students," Cassandra snapped. "It's just a formality, okay? Don't go all morbid on us now."

Since Ashley and Troy had finished their forms,

too, only Samantha was holding out. "All right," she agreed reluctantly. "But I don't like it."

"You don't have to do this," the woman said. "It's purely voluntary. And your friend's right, this is just one of those things we have to do. Government regulations to make sure we have more work than workers."

As soon as Samantha had signed, Cassandra dragged her through the doorway and into the main body of the hall. She'd been expecting to see professorial types, small booths and people guessing the lay of packs of cards. So she was surprised by what was actually there.

The room was about sixty feet long and forty wide, with a stage at the far end. That was curtained off and not in use. In fact, most of the space was empty. About ten feet from the door was another table with clipboards, manned by another grad student. Behind him was a mess of electronic equipment on several benches. They seemed to be wired together, and resembled Dr. Frankenstein's garage sale. Maybe Samantha might know what the machines were, but to Cassandra, they were simply machines. Some had screens that were lit up; others were just messes of plug-in wires that trailed all over. At the far end of the apparatus was a chair. Over it was positioned what looked like a hair dryer with a bad wiring job.

"Whoa!" Troy exclaimed. "It looks like we're in the beauty parlor by mistake!"

The grad student grinned. "You're the tenth person so far that's cracked that joke." He held out the clipboards. "Okay, guys, fill out the forms to the best of your abilities. Write on only one side of the paper at a time. Then keep them and take a seat." There were two rows of seats close to the hair dryer, and only two seats were taken.

Cassandra and her friends each took a pad and started to work down the questions. Most were biographical, and simple to fill out. One asked: "Do you believe in hunches?" and another: "Do you read your horoscope?" Some seemed designed to see how credulous they were, and others to see if they were skeptics. Cassandra was pretty much skeptical of most things in life, and said so. The only thing she believed in implicitly was herself. Then she watched what was happening.

One of the two people who had been in front of them had been taken to the chair. It was a boy she vaguely knew, but his name wasn't worth remembering. He sat down, a little nervously, and two more students stuck wires to his skull with suction cups or something. There was an elderly man handling the machinery, and a fifty-something woman with a severe case of bad hair watching the boy. She murmured something to him, and then tapped the computer keyboard beside her.

One of the machines seemed to be doing something, but Cassandra had no idea what. After a moment, the woman looked up. "Negative," she announced. "Okay, unhook him." The two students took the wires off his head, and smiled politely at him as he got up and left.

This didn't look as though it was going to be as much fun as she'd hoped, Cassandra realized. Actually, it looked kind of dull. But she'd never admit that to Samantha, who'd gloat over being right. Instead, she'd just have to sit through it, and pretend to be fascinated.

The other boy ahead of them went next. He had the sticky wire routine, and the bored "Negative," too, before he left. Then the woman came over to where the four of them were sitting.

She held out her hand, and took each of the clipboards. "Right," she said. "Just a few words of explanation. I'm Dr. Reese, from the university. I've been trying to do a study of where in the brain so-called psychic phenomena might originate. You know—telepathy, clairvoyance, ESP, that kind of thing. I've run tests on some professional psychics and discovered a small but interesting amount of odd electrical activity in one part of the left lobe of the brain. So now I'm trying to see if this kind of activity is present in other people, and, if so, whether they have increased evidence of psychic ability." She glanced at the forms. "Okay, let's start with Samantha, shall we?"

Samantha groaned, as if she'd been expecting that. Perhaps she had. With an accusing glance at Cassandra, she allowed herself to be led over to the apparatus. She looked very unhappy as the wires were attached to her forehead. Then Dr. Reese played with her keyboard, and the machinery seemed to hum to life.

Dr. Reese looked startled. "Positive," she murmured.

"What?" Samantha tried to twist her head to look

at the woman. The grad students yelped, so she stopped moving. "You've got to be kidding me."

Cassandra stared at her friend. Samantha was *psychic?* This was too cool!

"It doesn't mean anything necessarily," Dr. Reese cautioned her. "But I'd like to run a few more tests on you after the others are done." She had Samantha released. "Right, Ashley next."

Sitting back down beside Cassandra, Samantha gave her friend a scowl. "Thanks a lot. Now I get to do more tests."

"Hey!" Cassandra was excited, even if Samantha wasn't. "You're *psychic,* amiga! This is just so neat! Do something clever."

"I'm tempted to punch you," Samantha growled. "Right now that seems like the right thing to do. And if I'm psychic, I've got to be right, haven't I?"

"Negative," Dr. Reese pronounced over Ashley's readings. "Right, Cassandra, let's have you."

Grinning, Cassandra hurried over, taking Ashley's place in the chair. It was still warm. She rested her hands on the arms while the two students stuck the wires to her head. They felt a bit clammy, but not unbearably so.

"Right," the guy said. "Try to blank your mind. That's probably not hard."

That annoyed her a little. What did he think she was? A bimbo? But she played along, trying not to think about anything.

There was a slight tingle in her skin around the wires.

And then the universe exploded.

CHAPTER 3

SAMANTHA WASN'T AT all happy to be in the hall. Honestly, some days she wondered why she ever let Cassandra talk her into doing these stupid things! Testing her psychic abilities, of all things! She didn't believe in such things. Astrology, ESP, all that stuff—it was nothing but pure nonsense. People believed in that kind of thing because they were stupid, not because it existed.

So being told *she* had traces of this psychic ability was something of a blow to her. Surely there had to be some mistake! She didn't even believe in the thing! But Dr. Reese seemed to be convinced that her machine was right. That annoyed Samantha. She glared at Cassandra as her friend was put into the chair, and hoped that she'd get the same fate that she'd suffered. It would serve Cassie right!

And then Cassie screamed and collapsed, and Samantha's mind went crazy. She was shocked, and scared, and dived forward without even thinking about it. She managed to get her arms around Cassandra, preventing her from slamming into the hard wooden floor, but she collapsed under the deadweight of her friend. The wires had torn free as Cassandra had fallen, and dragged some of the equipment down. One of the grad students grabbed it before it could hit Samantha.

Then there were helping hands all around, reaching for both of them. Somebody took Cassandra's weight off Samantha, and somebody else helped her to her feet. Samantha was suddenly aware of the noise all around her.

"—an ambulance!" Dr. Reese was yelling as she bent to feel for Cassandra's pulse. "Now!" One of the students took off at a run.

"Cassie!" Troy was calling, as if desperate to wake her up. Ashley was standing ineffectually by, wringing her hands in shock.

"Huh?" Samantha said as somebody shook her. It was the woman with the forms. "What?"

"I asked if you were okay," the woman said, concern and shock on her own face.

"Me? I guess so." Samantha hadn't really thought about it. "What about Cassie?" She stared down at her friend. Dr. Reese had lowered her to the floor, and Cassandra's face was ashen.

Dr. Reese glanced up. "Her pulse is strong, but a bit fast. Did somebody go for the ambulance?"

Samantha bent down again as her mind started to function. "What happened to her?" she demanded.

"I don't know," Dr. Reese admitted. "That's never happened before."

"She must have gotten a shock from your equipment," Troy said accusingly.

"No!" Dr. Reese exclaimed. "It's fully shielded. That's completely impossible! I don't know what happened, but it wasn't our fault."

"Right," said Samantha. "It was somebody else's, huh?"

"Maybe she just fainted," the grad student suggested. "She's kind of skinny, maybe bulemic?"

"She is *not* bulemic," Samantha snapped. "She's just naturally thin. And she was fine until you wired her up and started your machine. Then she screamed."

"It's not my fault," Dr. Reese started again. The elderly man, a university professor named Charlton, intervened.

"Let's worry about whose fault it is after the young girl's been seen to," he said practically. "Dorothy, until we know, I think you should shut down your apparatus and call off the rest of today's tests."

Dr. Reese considered for a moment and then nodded. "Right, of course." She stood up and moved to do this. Samantha took her place beside Cassandra, rubbing her friend's wrist and praying that she would be okay.

"I don't understand," Dr. Reese said softly. Samantha looked up, and saw her staring at her machines. "The circuit boards are fried!"

"There *was* a power surge!" Troy said. "I knew you jerks were responsible! You're going to get sued for this."

"But the power surge came *after* she screamed," Dr. Reese insisted, "and it burned out all of my circuits."

Samantha stared at the scientist, and then at her friend. She prayed Cassie would be okay.

"I'm sure she's going to be fine."

Cassandra squeezed Mrs. Baker's hand in relief. Cassandra's mother gave a gasp, and squeezed back. They both moved forward to talk to the emergency room doctor. Samantha had called Cassandra's mother as soon as they'd arrived at the hospital, and she'd rushed over, panicking. Well, that was understandable. They'd only had each other since Mr. Baker had filed for divorce, and Cassandra and her mother were very close. It had been a painful wait until the doctor had emerged.

"What happened to her?" Mrs. Baker demanded. "Is she awake? Can I see her?"

The young man raised a hand. "One question at a time, please. Yes, she's awake, and yes, you can see her in a minute. First thing, though: I don't know what made her black out like that. She seems a little fuzzy on the details herself, which is probably only to be expected. The thing is that girls her age often have . . . incidents of sorts. Dizziness, anemia, that kind of thing. Maybe even heatstroke. I'd suggest that you take her to her own doctor tomorrow for a thorough checkup, but there doesn't seem to be very much the matter with her."

Mrs. Baker nodded, and Samantha was tremendously relieved. She'd been afraid that Cassandra had been injured by that crazy experiment. The doctor allowed them into the emergency room now, where Cassie was in a small room off to one side. Two nurses were putting away the test apparatus, and Cassandra was lying on a small bed. She grinned weakly at her mom and friend.

"Sweetheart!" Mrs. Baker exclaimed, rushing to her side. "Are you okay? The doctor said you are, but—"

"I'm okay, Mom, honest," Cassandra assured her. "Just a bit dizzy, that's all." She looked at where there was a Band-Aid on the inside of her elbow. "Probably due to blood loss for their silly tests." She focused on Samantha. "Hi, Sammy. Thanks for looking after me."

Samantha shrugged. "I told you it was a bad move to go to that quack scientific test."

"Maybe I should listen to you more," Cassandra answered.

"That'll be the day," Samantha muttered. But she gave her friend a reassuring smile. "So, are they letting you out of here, or are you staying the night?"

"I'm not staying," Cassandra said firmly. "I hate the way hospitals smell. That'll make you sick, even if you're well to begin with."

That was an opinion Samantha shared. She hated the stench that always filled hospitals. She glanced around and saw one of the nurses. "Can Cassie go home now?"

The nurse nodded. "The doctor's signed the discharge papers," she said. "And all the insurance forms have been filled out. Just make sure she's up to travel. It's probably a good idea to keep an eye on her tonight."

"And bed when we get home," Mrs. Baker added firmly.

Cassandra sighed. "Just what I wanted to do tonight," she muttered.

It wasn't as bad as Cassandra had feared. Samantha had gone home and wheedled permission from her mom for a sleepover. She'd then hurried around to the Baker house with her overnight bag. It was only seven, but Mrs. Baker had insisted on Cassandra going straight to bed, and was making the obligatory chicken noodle soup. Samantha was amazed to discover that she had an appetite.

Samanatha had always liked Cassie's room. It was much cheerier than her own. It had a canopy bed, all greens and golds, in which Cassandra sat as if holding court. Samantha had dropped her bag off in the spare room that would be hers for the night, and then gone to her friend. Mrs. Baker brought them the soup, and stayed to make sure Cassie actually ate it. After that, still worried, she left the girls together.

"How are you feeling?" Samantha asked, concerned. She took Cassandra's hand and squeezed it. "We were so scared for you."

Cassie thought for a moment. "It was really weird. I mean, there was just this moment of intense pain. Like somebody had set every nerve in my body on fire. And then I blacked out." She shook her head. "Then I had this really bizarro dream . . . and then I woke up in the hospital, getting the lab rat treatment."

"You don't hurt now?" Samantha demanded, worried.

"No, nothing." Cassie frowned. "Just a sort of buzz in my head. Like tinnitus or something. Do you know what happened? Was it Dr. Reese's machine?"

"*She* says not," Samantha said. "But that could just be her fear of lawsuits. Something went really wrong and fried all of the circuits. You must have had some of the power go through you, I guess."

"Maybe." Cassandra shrugged. "But I feel pretty much okay. And I never even got to find out if I'm psychic. I am *so* envious of you!"

"Don't be," Samantha said firmly. "I think that Dr. Reese is an absolute quack. She probably couldn't tell a psychic if one was reading her tea leaves."

That made Cassandra laugh, and they changed the subject. A little later, Troy called, and Samantha left her to talk to him alone on her bedroom phone. He did seem to be worried about Cassie, and Samantha was sure her friend would exploit that to the max. She went downstairs to see if she could help Mrs. Baker with anything.

"What actually happened today?" Cassandra's mother asked. She listened quietly while Samantha told her, a slight frown on her face. "Do you think that this university professor did something to Cassie?" she asked.

"I don't know," Samantha replied. "It's possible. Something messed up her equipment, but she says it was external. I think she's just covering her backside, to be honest. She didn't seem to have any more idea of what went wrong than the rest of us."

"I'll give her a call in the morning," Mrs. Baker decided. "She's going to have some explaining to do. And so does that university, unless they want to be sued."

"Sammy!!!!"

Samantha raised an eyebrow. "I think I'm being paged," she laughed, and headed back upstairs. Cassandra was waiting impatiently. "So, have you pried Troy out of Ashley's clutches yet?"

"No, but I'm working on it." Cassandra grinned. "Hey, why don't we test your psychic abilities?"

"Because I don't have any." Samantha's good mood was starting to evaporate. "And, like I said, I don't think we should mess with stuff like that."

"Maybe you're right," Cassie said. "But humor me just this once, huh?"

"Just this once?" Samantha glared at her. "I humor you all the time."

"Then don't break the habit of a lifetime, okay?" Cassandra grinned again, refusing to allow Samantha to say no and mean it. "There's a pack of cards in the top left drawer over there." She gestured at her vanity.

Sighing, Samantha went and got the cards. She

could never say no to Cassandra, no matter how silly or potentially embarrassing the request. Cassie seemed to be happy to be getting her own way, as always, and shuffled the cards.

"Okay, this is real easy," she announced. "I just turn the card over and look at it. Then you try to guess what it is. Didn't you say that the odds were one in five of being right?"

"That's with the Rhine deck," Samantha pointed out. "With a normal deck of cards, the odds are one in fifty-two of getting the right card."

"Oh." Cassandra obviously didn't care much. "Well, let's start. You stay at the bottom of the bed and guess when I look at the card." She drew the first card and stared at it.

Samantha sighed. "This is really dumb."

"Just *guess*," Cassie insisted.

"The two of spades," Samantha said, without even thinking. She couldn't wait for Cassandra to get bored with this game.

Cassie flipped the card down.

The two of spades . . .

A chill ran right through Samantha's body as she stared at the card. *She'd guessed it correctly!* But that *had* to be impossible. Her mouth went dry. Cassandra picked up the next card.

"Guess."

Samantha shook her head. "I don't want to do this."

"Guess."

She couldn't possibly be doing this! It was just a fluke, nothing to get nervous about! "Jack of hearts," she said before she could even think about it. Cassie shot her a look, and Samantha felt a second of triumph. Until Cassandra flipped the card.

The red jack smiled up at her.

"Again." Cassandra had another card in her hand.

Samantha *really* didn't want to do this. But Cassie wouldn't let her back out. Anyway, she couldn't possibly keep going like that. It was just dumb luck. What else could it be? "Seven of hearts."

It was.

Feeling something like shock, Samantha reeled off card after card, not even thinking about them. And she got every single card right. Every one of them . . .

"This is impossible," she finally blurted out. "Cassie, *nobody* has ever scored a hundred percent on this sort of test! Nobody!"

"Then I guess you've made the *Guinness Book of Records*," Cassandra said remorselessly. "You really *do* have psychic powers! This is so cool!"

"Cool?" Samantha shook her head. "Cassie, I don't want this! I don't even believe in it! It scares me."

"Fraidy cat," Cassandra scoffed. "Hey, we could make a killing at this. Have you ever tried playing the lottery? We could become rich!"

"I don't want to become rich," Samantha objected. "I want to be *normal*."

"Normal's boring, kiddo," Cassie assured her. "I'd stick with rich and famous if I were you. You could become astounding."

Samantha's heart was almost breaking. *Why me?*

she wondered. *What have I done to be so cursed?*
She didn't want to be psychic. She just wanted to be
Samantha Marlowe, normal girl. Why couldn't Cassie *see* that? Because, of course, Cassie would get a
huge kick out of being psychic. She just adored being
the center of attention, and couldn't understand why
anybody else felt differently. But Samantha didn't
feel that way at all.

"Let's give it a rest," she said weakly. "Cassie, I
really don't like this."

Cassandra shrugged. "Have it your own way," she
agreed amiably. "I think you're missing out on a gold
mine here, though."

They got through the evening somehow, though
Samantha knew she wasn't much fun. She couldn't
get that grim run of accurate guesses out of her
mind. How had she managed that? Why did she have
this ability? And how could she get rid of it? Eventually, Mrs. Baker insisted on bed for both of the
girls, and Samantha was only too happy to comply.
She gave Cassandra a hug and a kiss on the cheek,
and then went to get ready for bed.

She lay awake for ages, her mind filled concern.
She sincerely believed that it was asking for trouble
messing about with anything occult. She eventually
fell into a restless sleep. Strange, dark objects
seemed to be lurking there, watching her. She was
scared, and felt as if she was being buried alive or
something. Formless objects were surrounding her,
and—

Samantha suddenly sat up straight in bed, instantly

awake. The vague fears and shadows of her dreams vanished. Instead, she felt a sudden wave of real panic as she heard Cassie screaming as if all of the devils in Hell were tormenting her.

CHAPTER 4

CASSANDRA WAS STANDING in some dark, miserable place. She wasn't sure just where it was, but there were walls of stone and brick around her, though the buildings had no roofs. The sky was bright, stars burning with unnatural light, shedding a glow over the landscape. Yet it wasn't a bright glow. It was as if the light was hiding whatever it fell upon, rather than revealing it. This didn't make any sense to Cassandra, but she felt that it was true somehow: that in the glow, there were things hidden—things that *wanted* to be hidden. She couldn't see anything, of course, but she could *feel* something. And then there were small noises, like clawed feet skittering over wooden floors. But whenever she looked, there was nothing directly to be seen. Only the faint glow of light, covering . . . whatever.

Feeling really uncomfortable, Cassandra started to walk, past the dark walls, away from the lurkers in the light. A wall blocked her way, so she turned to continue sideways. Another wall blocked that way, so she turned and moved again. There didn't seem to be any logic to the way these buildings were made.

And there were neither doors nor windows in the walls. How were people supposed to get into them? Cassandra was feeling more and more apprehensive as she walked. Another blockage, another turn.

And more noises, this time from just beyond the walls. What was in this place with her? She stopped and listened. It sounded like something moving, but it wasn't clear. The wall had to be muffling the noise. She started walking again, darting glances all around her, disturbed by everything.

Another wall in front of her, and a choice of two directions to take. Which way should she go? This place was like a maze . . .

A maze.

It wasn't *like* a maze, it *was* a maze! That's what she had been trying to realize! She was in some kind of maze, trapped, forced to run it. For what? A piece of cheese? Some other reward?

And who—or what—was making her do this? She could sense *things* out there, watching her, studying her, waiting . . .

Cassandra was scared and angry. She wasn't a rat, to be tested like this! "I have my rights!" she yelled out to her unseen watchers. "You can't make me do this!" She refused to move another step. That would show them!

Oh yes we can . . .

Cassie *felt* rather than heard this reply, and it shook her up terribly. She whirled around. "Who's there?" she screamed, fighting hysteria. "What do you want of me?"

Run.

She whirled around again, but there was nothing to be seen. Whoever was doing this wasn't showing themselves. But she could hear something. The sound was coming from the path she'd already taken. Scratching noises, as if something large was moving.

Cassandra screamed. From around the last corner she had turned, a huge insect crawled. It was like some immense cockroach, ten or twelve feet long. Too many legs moved it forward, and its antennae twitched as it focused on her. Immense mandibles snapped together.

Cockroaches ate anything . . .

Your only chance is to run, the voice told her. It didn't sound pleased, or any other emotion. It was simply a fact, and Cassandra knew it was true. If she stayed where she was, she'd be caught and eaten by the grotesque creature.

She whirled and ran blindly. She didn't care where she went, as long as she managed to escape from that thing that was after her. She ran, staggered, fell against one wall, righted herself, and continued to run. And all the time she could hear the thing behind her.

Cassandra was sweating like crazy, her hair plastered to her head and neck, sweat streaming down her limbs. She brushed it from her eyes, trying to see where she was going. Her clothing stuck to her skin. Her bare feet slapped against the filthy streets.

She didn't know whether or not she was escaping from the monstrous insect. She didn't dare look back, in case it was getting closer and closer, those giant mandibles ready to snip off her head. She just ran and ran.

Until she slammed into something that gave way. Cassandra stopped, panting, and stared at what she had hit. Then she screamed again.

It was a body hanging from a pole, a thin rope around its neck. It was a teenage girl, her features all twisted out of shape. She had dark hair that hung lifelessly halfway down her back, and blue eyes that were bloodshot now. She would have been pretty alive, but now she was swinging, dead, from a pole. The body was twisting slightly because of Cassandra's running into it, but every detail was burned into her mind. The dark skirt, the yellow top, the sandals on her feet. Cassandra knew she'd never be able to forget them.

The monster! She'd forgotten about the insect while she was being so disgusted and shocked. She spun around, but there was now no sign of it. Maybe it had taken a wrong turn somewhere, and she was free of it. Maybe.

She glanced back at the poor girl's body, wanting to throw up. She felt sorry for whoever this had been, and repelled by the bloated corpse. She had to get away from it.

And then it began. Her nerves tingled, and Cassandra could feel hatred from somewhere rolling over her like a wave. With a sob, she fell to her knees as if she were praying to the corpse as the emotion battered at her frightened mind. Strong, primal, vindictive hatred. Hatred that had been directed at the girl, but was now being focused on Cassandra. She whimpered again as she felt the strong grip of the paralyzing force. Then she screamed as the hatred started to burn at her mind and her nerves. It was as if acid were being poured over every inch of her skin. She was on fire from the force of the hatred directed against her. She screamed and screamed—

—and woke up abruptly. Samantha was shaking her strongly. "Cassie! Cassie! Wake up!"

"I'm awake," she mumbled. "Don't do that."

Samantha stopped shaking her, and Cassandra sat there in her bed, bewildered. She was soaked in sweat, just as in her dream, and she was as exhausted as if she'd really been running all of those miles. There was a movement at the door, and her mom came in, brushing her hair out of her eyes and looking really concerned.

"Sweetheart, what's wrong?" She came to join Samantha at the side of the bed.

Cassandra tried to focus her thoughts. "Just a dream," she admitted. "A bad one. Giant bugs, dead bodies, the usual fun stuff. I'll be okay in a minute."

Mom nodded and patted her hand. She scowled. "Grief, you're soaked. You must have been too warm with that comforter on, honey."

It wasn't that, of course, but Cassandra didn't feel like explaining it. She glanced at the clock. Five in the morning . . . Well, she wasn't going to get any more sleep tonight, that was for sure. "I'll take a shower," she said. Nice warm water running all over her body was just what she needed right now. "I'll be fine, honest."

Mom nodded, and wandered off to bed again. She didn't have to be up for another couple of hours, and normally you just couldn't wake her at all. Samantha sat there, looking at her in concern.

"You sure you're okay?" she asked. "Cassie, you sounded really scared."

"Believe me, I was, Sammy." She shivered at the memory of it. She told her friend what she could remember of the dream. "I had something like it when I blacked out earlier," she confessed. "The bit about walls and the hidden things watching me. This was a lot worse. And that hatred I could feel . . . like something had examined me, and felt toward me what I feel toward a centipede or something. Like it thought I was disgusting and loathsome and it wanted to squish me underfoot."

"Well," Samantha said dryly, "all I dreamed about was being on the beach with a bunch of hunks in Speedos. Can't you have any *good* dreams?"

"Not today, it seems." She threw back the covers. "I'm going to get that shower and then get ready for school. I can't sleep again after all that."

"I can imagine." Samantha yawned and stretched. "Okay, I'll take the bathroom after you. Maybe we can make your mom breakfast for a change."

The shower felt really good. The needle spray hammered into her body, washing away the sweat and the negative feelings. Cassandra had always loved water, feeling its cleansing powers. She used the body shampoo liberally, getting rid of her shakes as well as sweat, and then washed her hair out. At least she had plenty of time today to dry it before school.

Samantha headed into the shower when Cassandra vacated it to get dressed. Cassie hurried down to the kitchen, and started a pot of coffee brewing. Mom couldn't get moving without two strong cups in the morning. "Brain fuel," she called it. Cassandra grabbed some milk, and then waited for Sammy to join her.

Briskly toweling her hair, Samantha came in a short while later. She was dressed for school, too, even though it was only six o'clock. She accepted a glass of milk with a smile, and sipped at it. "Feeling better?" she asked.

Cassandra started to comb out her hair, enjoying the feeling of the tines through her long tresses. "Yes," she said cheerfully. "It was so dumb of me to be so scared of a silly dream. I feel fine now." She heard the sound of a car outside, and then a thump in the driveway. "Mom's paper," she said. "It's a bit early today."

"I'll get it," Samantha volunteered. Dropping the towel in her chair, she dashed outside.

Cassandra continued to dry her hair, and then felt faint. She clutched the back of the closest chair and closed her eyes.

Broken buildings, jutting up through flames... people screaming, and running...

She gasped as the images flitted through her mind, and then everything was normal again. Shaking, Cassie wondered what had happened to her. Was it just a vivid dream fragment, half remembered from the night? Or something else?

Then Samantha was back, pulling the paper from the plastic bag it came in. "Oh, great," she said, staring at the front page.

"What?" Cassandra wasn't really interested, but Sammy sounded really bugged.

"Another dead girl," Samantha answered. "The third this year. She was found yesterday." She turned the paper so that Cassandra could see it.

It was the girl from her dream. Same face, same eyes. Same top and dark skirt...

Cassie went white. The milk glass fell from her fingers and smashed on the floor.

"Cassie!"

Cassandra shook her head, coming out of her state of shock. Her cheeks felt cold, and her hands were shaking. Her stomach was knotting up. "That girl..." she whispered. "It's the one from my dream."

"Huh?" Samantha looked at the picture again. "She's from Garrow, sixty miles away. You don't know her."

"No, but I *saw* her," Cassandra replied hollowly. "In my nightmare. The same girl, even the same clothes. I saw her *dead*. And now she *is* dead."

Samantha was struggling. "It's just some crazy co-incidence," she insisted.

"Like you guessing all the cards in a row?" asked Cassandra. "Sammy, *something* is happening here. I just wish I knew what . . ."

Samantha laughed, a rather brittle sound. "Cassie, that's my line. You're usually the one that says what I'm going to say. It's impossible. It was just a dream. Nothing more. It's just a coincidence."

"That's easy for you to say," Cassandra muttered. "You didn't have the dream."

"It's no big deal," Samantha insisted. "Look, we'd better get that glass cleaned up. Come on." She forced Cassandra to help her, and together they tidied it up. The whole time, Cassandra was shaking badly. It didn't matter what Sammy thought; *she* knew.

The girl was the one she'd dreamed about. The one killed by hatred, and swinging from a tree. It was the same girl. It *was*.

School would have been unbearable, except Cassandra was on autopilot all day. She was vaguely aware that Troy asked her how she was doing, and that she'd lied and said she was okay. She saw Ashley was with him. Other than that, the whole day was a long, dreadful blur. Everything kind of melted together in her mind and fused with snatches of visions.

Was she going crazy? Without warning, it was as if everything changed around her and she was looking out on a desolate landscape filled with burning houses and screaming people. Then reality would return, leaving her shaking.

After school, Dr. Reese was waiting outside for her and Samantha. That brought Cassandra out of it. She stared at the scientist.

"I have to talk with you," Dr. Reese snapped. "My equipment is ruined. The whole system just shorted out. Some tremendous influx of power from somewhere. Not the electricity, that's for sure. I checked with the company. It looks like it had to have come from *you*."

"That's impossible," Samantha interrupted flatly. "Cassie couldn't have caused that much static electricity."

"I don't think it was electrical power," Dr. Reese answered. "I think it was some sort of psychic overload. The apparatus registered a strong positive for Cassandra just before the circuits were all fried. And before she . . . blacked out. A lot stronger even than yours."

"Stronger than mine?" Samantha blinked several times fast. "That might explain the card business last night."

"What card business?" Dr. Reese asked eagerly.

"I got her to try to predict what cards I was holding," Cassandra explained. "She got them all right."

"All?"

"All," Samantha said. "I thought that was really freaky, but if Cassandra is stronger than me . . ."

"You might have some kind of psychic connection," Dr. Reese agreed. "Yes. Sometimes things like that occur between friends. One knows what the other is thinking, or if the other is in trouble. That sort of thing."

"Or the card I'm holding in my hand?" asked Cassandra.

"Quite." Dr. Reese rubbed her hands together. "This is all rather exciting. I want to examine the two of you. We have to test this bond, find out just what you're both capable of."

"No," Cassandra said instantly, and heard Sammy's echo of the same word. She glanced at her friend.

"I think it's wrong and dangerous to go into this," Samantha said firmly. "Testing it isn't something we should be doing."

"But this is for science," Dr. Reese pleaded, holding her hands out as if begging. "It's valuable research. If we can find out how you two do it, then—"

"Then you can get others to do it too?" Samantha suggested. "No thanks. I don't want other people doing this too. I don't even want us doing it!"

"For once," Cassandra said slowly, "I agree with you completely, Sammy." She shivered. "I think I touched . . . *something* out there," she tried to explain. "Something that isn't human. That doesn't like humans, the way we don't like bugs. That would stomp us flat into the floor if it could. But it doesn't understand us yet, so it can't hurt us." She knew she was groping for words to try to express something she didn't comprehend. It was obvious that she wasn't getting through.

"What are you talking about?" the scientist demanded. "You girls . . . This is sheer superstition talking! You sound like you've stepped right out of the Middle Ages, and you think this is witchcraft I'm talking about here! This is *science,* the advancement of the human race."

"No," Cassandra answered. "That's wrong. We can't do this. We have to stop, not go on."

Dr. Reese stared at her in disgust. "You're crazy," she said. "Your fears are taking control of you. You have to understand the importance of what I'm doing!"

"And you have to understand the importance of what I'm saying!" Cassandra screamed back. Abruptly, she realized that everyone around was staring at her as if she were demented or something. Her cheeks burned with embarrassment as she realized suddenly how she sounded. She could almost feel their laughter, like a solid thing. And the scorn pouring out of Dr. Reese. And the woman's frustration.

How could these stupid girls be so important and not understand?

Cassandra reeled away from the doctor in horror. She hadn't heard the doctor *say* that! It was more like she was picking up on what Dr. Reese *felt.* But she could sense those feelings really strongly. Just as she'd sensed the hatred from that . . . *thing* in her dream.

What was happening to her? She felt a grip on her elbow, supporting her. Cassandra looked around wildly, and saw that it was Sammy. She clutched her friend in panic, and felt her emotions, too, stronger than the rest: compassion, love, and worry. The power of these positive emotions gave Cassandra her strength back. With a deep breath, she managed to stand upright again.

She turned to face Dr. Reese. She could feel the disgust and irritation, but it was weaker than before and it didn't hurt as much. "We can't help you," Cassandra said firmly. "I don't even know if we can help ourselves." Then she turned her back on the stunned and furious woman.

Again, there was a flash of panic, and she was staring out at a landscape littered with ash and backlit by burning fires. She gasped, and blinked, and she was looking at Dr. Reese once again. "Come on, Sammy," she begged. "Help me get home. I'm really not feeling well." She felt a spike of pain and concern from her friend.

"Should we get you to the hospital again?" Samantha asked.

"No," Cassandra answered. "There's nothing that they can do for me. I'm in serious trouble, and you may be the only one who can help me right now. We have to get me home, fast."

What was happening to her?

CHAPTER 5

SAMANTHA HAD BEEN thinking—well, maybe more like *praying*—that things wouldn't get any weirder. It looked as if she'd lost out on that hope. She sat beside Cassandra on her friend's bed and stared at her. "You say you've started to feel other people's emotions now?"

"Yes."

Samantha winced. "You're making it sound like you've turned into some sort of . . . psychic supergirl or something. Don't you realize that this sounds really . . ." She groped for a polite word.

"Insane?" Cassandra suggested. "Don't you think I know that? Sammy, I'm *scared*. I don't want to be able to do this. I could feel what Dr. Reese felt, and when the kids started to laugh at me, I could feel their derision and contempt, and it *hurt*. Thank God you're my friend, because it was only that strength that kept me going."

Samantha didn't know what to say to comfort Cassandra, so she took her hand. "Listen, maybe we should take you to a doctor or something." She was tempted to say "psychiatrist," but bit it back.

"I know you're worried about me, Sammy," Cassandra answered. "I can feel it. But going to a shrink wouldn't help me. I don't know how to stop what's happening to me."

Cassie had picked up on Samantha's unspoken thoughts anyway. It was probably pointless to hide them. They had already proven that there was some sort of psychic link binding them together.

"I was afraid that something bad would happen," Samantha confessed. "But nothing like this ever occurred to me. Look, why don't you get some rest? Maybe it'll get better."

"Better?" Cassandra laughed bitterly. "Sammy, how could it get worse? I've seen somebody's death, and now I'm picking up people's emotions and they're affecting me. You were so right to try to stop me from going to that place. Why didn't I listen to you?"

Samantha smiled wanly. "Cassie, you've *never* listened to me. You just do what you want, and don't hear anything that anyone says that goes against it."

"I know." Cassandra sighed. "And now I'm being punished for it. I *can't* ignore people anymore. Their emotions affect me directly."

"Maybe it's just a temporary thing," Samantha said hopefully. "You know, like a minor power overload. It'll probably wear off in a few days."

"God, I hope so."

Samantha was worried, because Cassandra sounded so depressed. This was really not like her at all. Normally nothing ever bothered her for long. She had one of those resilient personalities. Even the time she'd broken her leg in fourth grade, she'd made a big joke out of it, and made everyone else laugh along with her. Now she was so down.

"You want me to sleep over again?" Samantha suggested. "I know my folks will be glad to have me out of the house. I don't know how your mom will feel about having to feed me two days in a row, though."

"I know how I'll feel." Cassandra smiled gratefully. "Thanks, Sammy. I really don't want to be alone too much."

"Okay," Samantha said. "I'll go get fresh clothes, and I'll be back in about twenty minutes. Isn't it your turn to cook tonight? I can help out, if you can stand it."

The evening went as well as could be expected. Cassandra was wrapped in gloom most of the time, and barely paid attention to whatever they watched on TV. Samantha kept sneaking glances at her friend, and saw that Cassie was lost in her thoughts and fears. She wished there was something she could do to help other than just sit around for moral support, but it was hard to figure out what was happening.

Finally, though, it was bedtime, and Samantha crawled between the covers with some relief. The evening had been a strain, and she had a slight headache. She'd seen Cassandra take a couple of headache pills, so it was obvious that they both had similar problems. Still, Samantha was sure things would work out well.

Until Cassie started screaming at five in the morning again.

Samantha shot, bleary-eyed, into her friend's room and shook her awake. Cassie wouldn't snap out of it, though. She was asleep, a deadweight, and soaked in perspiration again, her honey hair plastered to her head. Samantha shook her again and yelled, trying to ignore the horrible screams in her ears. Mrs. Baker staggered in, looking shocked.

"What's wrong?" she asked, as Cassandra screamed and screamed in her sleep.

"I can't wake her up!" Samantha said desperately. "She's having a really bad dream, and she won't snap out of it."

Mrs. Baker looked at her daughter with fear in her eyes. "I'd better call an ambulance," she decided, and started to leave the room.

Cassandra suddenly opened her eyes and stopped screaming. Her body went tense, and Samantha let her go.

"It's Ashley," Cassandra said in a soft voice. "She's dead."

"What?" Samantha stared at her friend. "Cassie, what are you talking about?"

Cassandra seemed to be coming back to them from an immense distance. "In my dream," she said, shaking, rubbing her own shoulders. "I saw her. Ashley. She was killed. Someone with a knife . . ." She whimpered.

Mrs. Baker pushed Samantha aside and hugged her daughter. "Hush, sweetheart," she murmured. "It was just a bad dream."

"No," Cassandra said with conviction. "It wasn't a bad dream. I saw it. I *felt* it. The person who killed her hated her. He wanted to tear her to pieces, blow by blow, and he tried. She screamed, but then she stopped, because she was dead. And he kept on cutting and cutting her . . ."

"Cassandra!" Mrs. Baker said firmly. "It was just a silly dream. It's not real. It didn't happen. Don't distress yourself over something that doesn't mean anything."

"Mom," Cassandra said, "it's real. I can't explain it, but it's true. I know it."

Mrs. Baker didn't know what to do, that was obvious. "You've been under some stress, haven't you?" she asked gently. "What is it, honey? Boy problems? School problems? Bullies?"

Cassandra gave a strangled laugh. "Don't I wish! I'd give anything if I could just say it was one of those things. But it isn't. I know you don't believe me. I can feel it. But it's true." She reached over to the pack of cards that were still sitting on the night table, and handed them to Samantha. Sammy took them without a word. "Shuffle them and look at them."

Samantha didn't want to, but she didn't have much choice. She shuffled the cards, and then started to turn the first one over.

"Six of diamonds," Cassandra said, before Samantha had even looked.

It was.

Cassandra continued, and called every single card correctly—before Samantha even looked at them. Mrs. Baker stared from one girl to the other.

"That's very clever," she said. "But it's just a trick."

"It's no trick, Mom," Cassandra said. "Look, go ahead, pick up a book from my desk. Open it anywhere you like, and read the first line you get to with your back to me. Go on." Her mother looked confused, but did as she said. After a moment, Cassandra said: "The road stretched out before her, bright with wildflowers and promises."

Mrs. Baker gasped, and slammed down the book. "How could you do that?" she asked.

"I don't know," Cassandra replied. "But I can. And it's getting worse. My mind's buzzing with it all, and I can't stop it." She looked at Samantha. "I had that dream about the maze again," she said. "And the things that watched me. I could feel their hatred even stronger this time. They want to destroy us, Sammy, and I'm afraid." She stared, hollow-eyed, at her pillow. "I'm afraid to go back to sleep, Sammy. *They're* waiting for me there . . ."

"I guess an early start to the day won't hurt any

of us," Mrs. Baker decided, trying to be cheerful. "I can make us all a batch of pancakes, if you like."

"Whatever," Cassandra answered without enthusiasm. She pawed at her sticky hair. "It looks like I'd better hit the shower again." She got to her feet and stumbled from the room.

Her mother looked at Samantha, concerned. "Is she going to be all right, do you think?"

"You know Cassie," Samantha said. "Nothing keeps her down for long. She'll bounce back from this, you just wait and see."

Mrs. Baker nodded, and then hurried off to start breakfast. She seemed to see food as the solution to all her daughter's emotional problems. Samantha went to the guest room, and grabbed her own toiletries. She really needed a hot shower, too.

She tried to wash off her own doubts and fears with the hot spray, but it didn't work. She didn't know what was worse: believing in Cassie or not believing. If she believed, then her friend was somehow being haunted, as well as cursed. If she didn't believe . . . well, then, Cassie had to be cracking up in the most spectacular fashion since Humpty Dumpty. Either way, it wasn't good.

She toweled off, and dressed in a hurry. Then she went outside.

The newspaper was there, sitting on the lawn.

It took all of her willpower and courage to pick it up, and then to slowly unfold it . . .

She gasped with relief. It was just some headline about a presidential scandal. She let out her breath—business as normal. She quickly scanned the paper, and the only thing in it about a killing was the inevitable follow-up to the poor girl of the other day. Nothing at all about Ashley. Feeling triumphant, she went back inside. Cassandra was at the kitchen table, ignoring the delicious smell of freshly made blueberry pancakes. "There's nothing about Ashley in the news," Samantha announced in relief. "Just the same old same old."

If she'd been expecting that to cheer Cassandra up, she was disappointed. "It happened," she said firmly. "Or it will happen. I know."

"Don't be so despondent, dear," her mother said, handing both girls plates of pancakes. "Eat your breakfast. It'll do you good."

Samantha ate readily enough, dunking her food in syrup. Cassie ate, but apparently without noticing what she was eating. At six-thirty, she jumped up and went to the phone. Samantha followed, puzzled.

"Oh, hi, Mrs. Curran," Cassie said, trying to sound cheerful. "Could I talk to Ashley, please?" There was a pause. "Oh, no, it's not important. I guess I'll catch her later at school. Thanks." She replaced the receiver and looked at Samantha. Her eyes were tired and red. "Ashley stayed at a friend's house last night. Mrs. Curran didn't seem to be bothered, and she said it was Paula Cook's."

"Then there's nothing to be worried about," Samantha said in relief. "If there had been any . . . bad news, her mother would have heard it. Your dream was wrong."

"Not wrong," Cassandra answered in a quiet voice. "Just ahead of its time."

"Look, Cassie." Samantha tried to snap her out of this mood. "We can just warn Ashley to be careful when we see her later at school, okay? It's not a problem."

"I hope to God you're right," Cassandra said. "But I don't feel at all sure of that."

What a start to the day! Samantha thought. Together, they headed for school. Samantha wasn't surprised and didn't say anything when Cassandra stopped by the main entrance, obviously intending to wait. She just stayed quietly with her friend, praying this whole thing was a false alarm. Her nerves were really getting strained, though, with the cold silence, when she spotted Paula arriving. Cassandra stiffened.

"Ashley's not with her," she said.

"Maybe she went home because she'd forgotten something?" Samantha suggested. "Look, Paula's laughing, so nothing bad could have happened, could it?"

"Couldn't it?" Cassandra threw herself into Paula's path. "Where's Ashley?" she demanded.

Paula looked annoyed. "Are you her keeper all of a sudden?" she asked.

"Where is she?" Cassandra yelled. "She slept over with you. Where is she?" Other students were pausing to stare at her. She was making a scene again, but didn't seem to be aware of it.

Paula scowled. "Look, it's none of your business," she said, definitely worried about something.

"Fine," Cassandra snapped. "I'm going to call the police."

"What?" Paula looked stunned. "Hey, there's no reason to overreact!" She tugged at her hair. "Okay, just between the three of us, all right?"

"Talk," Cassandra snarled.

Paula glanced around and lowered her voice. "Ashley wasn't with me last night. We just told her mom that so she wouldn't worry. She was with Troy."

"Troy?" Samantha stared at Paula. "How come?"

"Boy meets girl, that kind of thing," Paula said, rolling her eyes. "They wanted to spend the time together, okay? Look, they're both old enough to know what they're doing."

"They're both absolute jackasses," Cassandra growled. "Just remember, *you're* responsible for what's happened to her."

"What could happen?" Paula asked, confused. "They were going to take precautions."

"There are some things you can't take precautions against," Cassandra said coldly. "Like that."

Samantha followed her friend's gaze, and stiffened in shock.

A police car was drawing up to the school.

"Stick around," Cassandra informed Paula. "They're probably looking for you."

"What do you mean?" Paula's voice was squeaky with fear.

Cassandra didn't reply. She just watched the policemen get out of the car and come toward them. Then she spoke to the lead policeman. "This is Paula Cook," she said. "You want to talk to her, don't you?"

The cop looked confused. "How could you know that?"

"I know too much," Cassandra said heavily. "It's Ashley, isn't it?"

The policeman stared at her sharply, suddenly alert. "You figured she was in trouble?" he demanded.

"Trouble?" Cassandra snorted. "She's *dead* isn't she?"

The two policemen exchanged glances. "And how could you possibly know that?" the first asked.

"I saw it," she replied softly. "In a dream."

Samantha grabbed her friend, sensing that Cassie was losing all of her strength. Her skin was ice cold, and she was shaking. Sammy was too numb to know what to think, but the police weren't.

"I think the three of you had better come with us," the first cop decided. "We're going to have to get to the bottom of this."

Samantha sighed. She'd been afraid of that. Cassandra should never have opened her mouth—but she was never smart enough to know when to keep it shut. She looked at the policeman. "Do you know who did it?" she asked.

"Oh, yes." The second cop spoke for the first time. "We caught the guy red-handed. Her boyfriend, Troy Webster."

Paula gave a gasp of shock, and even Samantha felt like screaming at that news . . .

CHAPTER 6

CASSANDRA FELT MORE numb than anything else for the next couple of hours. The police were more than puzzled by her, and struggled to make some sense out of what she was telling them. They couldn't accept that she had seen it in a dream, and couldn't figure out how she could possibly have known about the murder unless she'd been present. But Troy had denied this, and Samantha had told them that the two girls had been together all night. Failing to make anything stick, the police had decided to label her a kook who'd made a lucky guess and then told her and Samantha to leave.

"I want some information first," Cassandra said firmly, ignoring the face that Samantha pulled. "Did Troy say *why* he killed Ashley? She was his girlfriend, and they seemed to be getting along fine. They were inseparable, and nobody I know ever even heard him say a bad word to her. It doesn't make sense that he'd suddenly decide to kill her. Are you sure he did it?"

The detective looked annoyed. "That's confidential, and a part of our investigation," he finally said.

Cassandra nodded. She had felt his emotions as he'd considered the question. "You don't know, do you?" she murmured. "He hasn't been able to explain himself why he did it."

The policeman glared at her. "How are you doing this?" he demanded. "Are you psychic or something?"

"You can rule out the *something*," Cassandra told him.

The detective shuffled nervously as this sank in. "We've worked with psychics in the past, but I'd need to get authorization from much higher up. Your best bet is to just go home."

Sammy took her arm. "He knows what he's saying," she urged. "Let's go, Cassie."

Cassandra knew that this would be the worst possible thing to do right now. She needed some answers, and the only way she'd get them was from Troy. Still, if the police wouldn't let her talk to him, there might be a use for her newfound abilities, after all.

"Can I just sit down for a few minutes?" she asked the cop, trying to inject all the sweetness she could into her smile. "I just need to gather my thoughts."

"Sure, kid." He gestured to a small waiting room. "I'll be back in five minutes."

Cassandra nodded, and collapsed into one of the chairs. Sammy glanced at her, clearly suspecting something. "I'm telling the truth," Cassie insisted. "I *do* have to gather my thoughts. Now, stay quiet for a minute." She closed her eyes and concentrated.

Yesterday, she'd felt the emotions flowing from Dr. Reese when the woman had confronted them. And she could feel the support from Sammy. How much harder could it be to reach out with her mind and feel the emotions that had to be raging inside Troy right now? She focused her thoughts, concentrating on Troy . . .

And then she had it. It wasn't sharp and clear, like the sort of telepathy that happened in science fiction stories. No words, as such, just emotions and moods. But they were clearly Troy's.

He was picturing what was supposed to have happened last night, going over the events in his mind. It was going to be their best date ever. He'd even made dinner reservations at a nice restaurant, and had a corsage in the fridge for her. He and Ashley had been in the kitchen, going for it, when he'd seen the knife, and picked it up, and—

Cassandra was stunned, feeling all of his emotions. He *didn't* know why he'd done it. He hated himself for it, and he was scared that he was mentally sick. He had loved Ashley, and couldn't understand why he had done what he had done. It made as little sense to him as to anyone else. He wanted to blot out everything, but couldn't.

Samanatha grabbed her arm. "Are you okay?" she asked anxiously. "You looked like you were going to faint."

"No, I'm not okay." Cassandra's voice was broken and shaky. "Sammy, he doesn't know why he did it. He was planning a romantic dinner for two, and instead, he saw a knife and just . . . did it."

"That doesn't make any sense," Samanatha objected. Cassandra noticed that she didn't say that she didn't believe what Cassie was claiming to have done.

"I can't help it!" Cassandra snapped. "That's how it is."

The policeman popped his head around the door. "You girls had better leave now," he said. "Come on."

"You'd better watch him carefully," Cassandra informed him. "He wants to kill himself from shame and loathing."

"Well, that's a point in his favor," the cop answered, obviously humoring her. He led them to where Samantha's father was waiting for them in the lobby.

"Dad will take us home," Sammy said gently.

Cassandra nodded. She was quiet, lost in her thoughts, until they reached the Marlowe house. She gratefully accepted the offer that she come in and have a cup of tea.

"What is it, Cassie?" Samantha asked when they were left alone.

"I saw what happened," Cassandra answered,

shuddering at the memories of Ashley being butchered that she'd picked up from Troy's shattered mind.

"God, that must have been awful." Sammy touched her arm gently. Strength flowed back into Cassandra.

"Worse than that." She stared at her friend. "Sammy, it was those creatures that I've been seeing in my dreams. They made him do it. They flooded him with hate, and made him turn on Ashley."

Samantha was stunned. "What? How?"

"I don't exactly know," Cassandra replied miserably. "But I'm scared that it's my fault. I don't think they even knew the human race was here until they contacted my mind. Now they hate us with a burning passion. They want to stomp us out. And they aim to do it through me!"

"Cassie, that's crazy!" Samantha gripped her arms and shook her. "It's not your fault. Even if what you say is true, the whole thing was an accident! It's not your fault!"

"Yes it is," Cassandra said bitterly. "I was such a fool to insist on going to that experiment! And now everybody is paying for it."

"Look, what happened to Ashley is horrible. And to Troy, too. But you can't let that affect you like this."

Cassandra stared at Samantha in horror. "Sammy, you don't understand! This was just their way of starting! They wanted to be sure they could do it— control people, make them do what these nightmares want. Now they know they can. And it's going to get worse! They're going to keep on going, until there's none of us left!"

Finally, Samantha started to understand what the real problem was, and she looked as appalled and terrified as Cassandra felt.

The *things* wanted to exterminate the human race. And it looked as if they had found their weapon.

Cassandra . . .

"It's all my fault," she whispered, tears trickling down her cheeks as she filled with shame and self-loathing at what she'd done. She had brought this plague onto the human race. Maybe she wasn't *seeing* what was happening as much as *causing* it. If she hadn't been so stupid, Ashley wouldn't be dead and Troy wouldn't be going crazy in prison.

It was all her fault. And it would only get worse. Through her, the lethal aliens had a foothold in the real world.

She had to stop them. And there was only one way to do that. Isolate them.

Cassandra managed a slight smile. "I've got to go to the bathroom," she said apologetically. "I'd better get home."

"Are you sure you're okay?" Samantha asked. Her concern and affection were like a blazing light, and Cassandra appreciated this.

"Yes," she lied. "I'll get over this. I'll be fine." She hugged her friend. "See you around."

She walked home, lost in her thoughts and fears. She was the conduit through which these creatures were working. There was only one way to stop them in their plans. She had to cut them off from this world once more. She had to stop their access. And *she* was their way in, so she was going to have to kill herself. It was logical, the only possible solution. Without her, those things couldn't get through.

In the bathroom, she opened the medicine cabinet. What was the fastest, best way to do it? Razor blade? No, it took too long, and Mom might come home and find her. Drug overdose? She didn't have a clue if they had anything that might do the trick. Neither she nor Mom liked taking medications, and, thankfully, never really needed any.

Poison . . . There were always lots of poisonous cleaning things. She winced at the thought of the pain she'd suffer. But better a little pain for her than annihilation for the human race. She found a bottle marked with the skull and crossbones, and opened the top.

Tears trickled down her face. She didn't want to do this, but it was the only way. Everybody had to be safe, and this was the way to make sure they were. She raised the bottle to her lips.

"No!"

Something hard slammed into her, and the bottle flew from her fingers. She crashed into the shower door, cracking it and sending a lancing pain through her left side. Cassandra howled, and realized that Sammy was there, panting hard and glaring furiously at her.

"What the hell do you think you're doing?" Samantha demanded.

"Stopping them," Cassandra explained painfully. "It's the only way."

"You *idiot!*" screamed Samantha. "That's what they *want* you to think!"

"What?" Cassandra couldn't understand her friend. She sat down on the toilet seat, rubbing her left shoulder. "What?"

Samantha knelt on the floor in front of her and grabbed her hand. "Cassie, I *knew* what you were going to do. Psychic link, remember? I'm not as strong as you, but even I could feel that you were going to kill yourself. And I could tell that *they* were behind it. Cassie, they want you dead! You're not their *link* here—you're their *enemy*! Now that they know the human race is here, they can come in at any time. They got through to Troy while you were nowhere near him—in fact, you were asleep at the time. If they want you dead, it's because you can hurt them somehow."

Cassandra realized that Sammy was right. She could *feel* their slimy presence in her mind, and understood that they *had* been trying to remove her. They hated her, as they hated all humans, but they were scared of her as well.

"It's okay, Sammy," she said, forcing her mind back on track. "They were trying to get me to kill myself. Maybe I *can* do something to stop them. That's why they wanted me dead. They know now they can reach the world without me, that they can make people do terrible things. They don't need me anymore."

"Right!" Samantha laughed wildly. "Cassie, stay

with us. Stay focused. If you can hurt them, or stop them, we have to figure out how."

"And we have to warn people," Cassandra added firmly. "People have to know what's going on. They have to know that their minds can be taken over, and that they can be flooded with hate. We have to make sure they are warned, and can fight back!"

Samantha shook her head. "Cassie, look, *I* believe you. I've known you all my life, and I trust you. But . . . well, this is going to sound totally flaky if you try to explain it to anybody else. They're going to lock you away in a psychiatric hospital if you try to tell people that we're all in danger of being murdered by aliens from some psychic dimension. A dimension that they have to take your word even exists. Can't you see that?"

"Yes," Cassandra answered. "I agree, there's a good chance I won't be believed. But what's the alternative? Let them live their lives thinking that everything is just fine until they each get murderous urges to kill whomever they love the most? Sammy, I know I'm going to have trouble convincing people, but anything's better than doing nothing! I have to try it." She stood up and headed for the door.

"Then I'd better come with you to pick up the pieces," Samantha said. "And I still think it's a stupid idea. Who are you going to tell?"

"The kids at school," Cassandra said. "They seem to be the most vulnerable. Plus, they know me, and they might just be more inclined to listen to me."

"Dream on," muttered Samantha, but she didn't try to stop her.

The cafeteria was crowded, but it was the best place for talking to as many people in one place as she could. Steeling herself, Cassie clambered onto one of the tables and yelled out: "Everybody quiet! Listen to me!" And she put every ounce of power she had into willing them to obey her. Maybe she had more presence than she had thought, or maybe the kids were just puzzled or in need of diversion. But they quieted down almost immediately, and everyone turned to look at her.

Swallowing, Cassie focused her thoughts, and refused to let failure be an option. "You've probably all heard by now that Ashley Curran was murdered last night," she said, and the room was hushed completely. She had everyone's attention now. "And that the killer was Troy Webster. Well, it's true, and Troy's in jail right now. But it wasn't his fault." Everyone was paying her silent, rapt attention now, and she forced herself to plunge on.

"There's an evil influence that forced him into that madness. And it's growing stronger. It's going to try to convince all of you to do similar acts of hatred and destruction. But you have to stop it. You've got to resist it with all of your might. Otherwise this town is going to turn into a slaughterhouse.

"Don't listen to the seductive whispers in your minds. Fight them! Stay strong! And watch out for your lives. Even if you can resist, there are going to be others who can't, and they will want to kill you. You've got to be strong and careful!"

A wave of weakness washed over her, and Cassandra staggered. Paula Cook stepped forward, radiating disgust and hatred. "You freak!" she yelled. "You knew about Ashley's murder before anybody else! You're some kind of sick freak! And now you're trying to get us to turn on each other!"

"No!" Cassie cried. "That's not what I'm doing at all! Believe me, I'm trying to help you all. To save your lives!"

"It's *your* fault!" Paula screamed back. "You were friends with Troy! And he killed *my* friend! You're just trying to get him off the hook! Well, it won't work!"

Cassie could feel the crowd turning against her now, but she couldn't stop. "No, please!" she cried frantically. "You must listen to me!"

"Must we?" called one student. "I don't think so, *freak!*" He grabbed some of the food from his plate and threw it at her. Spaghetti slapped across her cheek, stinging.

"Freak!" one of the girls howled. The cry was taken up, and then food began to pelt Cassie from all directions. It stung, it stuck, and it hurt. But not as much as the wave of dark emotions that rocked Cassie. She fell, filthy, onto the table surface. Some of the nearest students spat at her.

"No!" she screamed. "Please!"

"You pervert!" Paula howled, emptying her soda in Cassandra's face. In seconds, the others joined in, showering her with soda.

Hands grabbed Cassandra, and she started to fight, until she realized that they belonged to Samantha. Stunned and barely able to focus, Cassie allowed her friend to drag her out of the jeering, howling mob.

A couple of other girls and two boys helped, shielding Cassie and Sammy as best they could.

In the hallway, Cassandra staggered, leaning against a wall, unable to go any further. She was covered in filth, drenched to the skin, and battered. It was her mind that hurt the most, though, rocked by the sheer loathing and hatred coming from the cafeteria.

"It's no good," Cassandra moaned. "They won't listen. The creatures are too strong, and they're using the kids' natural mind-sets to push them along. I can't get through to them."

Samantha nodded. "Yes. Now what do we do?"

Cassandra turned haunted eyes to her friend. "Pray that some will survive. There's nothing else we can do right now." And she fled into unconsciousness to escape the pain.

CHAPTER 7

SAMANTHA CAUGHT CASSIE as she collapsed, grunting under the strain. "This is getting to be a habit," she muttered. "A very bad one." The boys helped her to lower Cassie gently to the floor.

"Was she . . . was she telling the truth? In there?" Samantha looked up. It was Connie asking. Her eyes flickered across the other students helping: Scott, Eric, Marie. She couldn't remember any last names, but they weren't important. "Yes," Samantha said firmly. "She was, no matter how crazy it sounded."

Scott swallowed. "If it were anyone else," he said slowly. "Actually, normally I'd include Cassie. I'd figure it was a joke. But nobody deliberately provokes that kind of antagonism just for a joke. And I know *you* would never go along with it. You don't have that much of a sense of humor."

"Gee, thanks," Sammy said dryly.

"What do we do now?" asked Marie.

"Get Cassie home again," Samantha decided. "But I don't want to carry her like this. We'll all get filthy."

"I can borrow my dad's car," Eric offered. "I kind of know how to drive."

"And we can get some sweats from the gym to cover Cassie's clothes," Connie suggested.

"Good thinking," agreed Samantha. "Go to it." Both of them shot off.

"We can't just leave school in the middle of the day," Scott objected.

"I think school's going to be out anytime," Samantha said. "Listen." They were silent for a short while, and they could all distinctly hear the sound of crash after crash in the cafeteria. "I think the natives are getting restless tonight."

"They're going to get in a lot of trouble," Marie muttered.

"Somehow, I don't think that will occur to them," Samantha said. "Those *things* Cassie was talking about seem to have inflamed their minds, setting them on a rampage."

Scott looked at the cafeteria doors, obviously worried. "Are we safe here?"

"Not for long," Samantha had to admit. Then she smiled as Connie came running back, a track suit in her hands. Quickly, the three of them struggled the pants and top on over Cassandra's ruined clothes. Then Samantha and Scott carried Cassie's unconscious body between them to the main door. Eric was waiting for them in his battered Thunderbird, and in moments they were speeding away from the school.

"I feel really bad about cutting school like this," Marie confessed. She had a reputation as a nerd, and seemed to want to live up to it.

"Trust me, our loss won't be noticed," Samantha assured them. "This is only going to get worse."

"Will it get better?" Connie asked anxiously.

Samantha sighed. She wished she hadn't been asked that. "I don't know. But the mind-things seem to be afraid of Cassie for some reason. Presumably because she can defeat them, even if we don't know how yet."

They arrived at the Baker house. Sammy used Cassie's key to let them all in. As they did so, Cassie groaned, and opened her eyes.

"Hi, guys," she muttered in a thick voice. "Am I too late for my own funeral?"

Samantha helped get her onto the couch. "Too early, thankfully. How do you feel, Cassie?"

"Like six people are hitting my head with bricks. From the inside." She rubbed a hand through her hair, and winced at the amount of sauce and spaghetti it dislodged. "What am I, dish of the day?"

"Well, you are kind of cute," Scott said, grinning. "But I wouldn't go that far."

"I'm going as far as the bathroom," Cassandra decided. Then she managed a weak smile. "I seem to be spending a lot of my time there lately. Back as soon as I don't drip food." She was a little unsteady on her feet, but determined.

Samantha used the time to fill the other four in on what was happening. They listened almost in silence. Obviously it was hard for them to take it all in, but they did their best.

"Nobody else is going to believe us," Scott said finally.

"They will soon," Samantha promised. "Listen." There was the far-off sound of police sirens. "I think the trouble is escalating."

"You're right," said Cassie, reentering the room. She'd showered and changed into jeans and a blouse, and was vigorously toweling her long hair. "When I was unconscious, I saw *them* again. They're focusing on the kids. They seem to be able to get through to them easier than adults right now. But their powers are growing stronger as they practice, and they'll be able to do whatever they like soon. They want to use our friends to start wiping out the human race."

"You've got to be kidding," Connie begged.

"I wish I was," Cassandra answered. "But I'm not. Those things have declared war on the human race. And I'm part of the problem."

"What do you mean?" Eric asked, confused.

"They found the Earth through me," Cassie explained. "And they followed me back here. I'm some sort of restraining force on them right now. I don't know how, but I can block them a little—as long as I'm awake. But when I go to sleep, or get knocked out, their powers increase." She looked haunted. "I've *got* to stay awake. It weakens them."

"But not enough to stop them," Samantha realized.

"No," Cassie agreed. "Not enough to stop them. But they *are* scared of me. Whatever gave me this power to get through to their dimension, or world, or whatever, also gave me the power to block them. The only thing is, I don't know how to do it!"

They considered this thought in silence. "Then how do we find out?" Scott finally asked.

"I don't know." Cassandra growled low in her throat. "God, for the first time, I wish I'd paid more attention to things. Maybe something would occur to me then!"

Samantha squeezed her friend's hand. "We'll manage," she promised, sounding a great deal more confident than she felt. "So, now what do we do?"

"We get out of here, for one thing," Cassandra said firmly. "Several of the kids at school know where I live. They're all getting worked up, and it won't be long before they decide to come after me. Those *things* want me dead before I can stop them. If I'm dead, the blockage is permanently removed, and they can flood this world with their hatred."

"My house?" Samantha suggested nervously.

"Same problem," Cassie answered. "We can't any of us go home—they're bound to look for us there. Let's just start moving. And let's do it *now!*"

She led the way out of the house, and then started down the street away from the school. Eric gestured at his car. "Why don't we take that?"

"Because the problem's spreading," Cassandra answered. "The center of infection seems to be the school right now. And that's where those police cars were heading. If they get control of some of the police, they could use them to order roadblocks. And a lot of people know what your car looks like."

Samantha's spirits sank even further. "You're not exactly reassuring me," she complained.

"I know. But we have to face facts." Cassandra led them in a tight group, and as they hurried through the streets, she stared at their four companions. "I wonder why you four weren't affected?"

"Well," Marie said, "I was affected. But I just knew it was wrong, and didn't act on it. Then the urge to attack you just went away."

"Same here," Scott agreed. "For a minute, I wanted to hurt you, but I knew that was crazy, so I wouldn't give in. Then I knew I had to help you."

Samantha considered this as Connie and Eric added the same testimony. "The things can only *influence* people," she said. "Push them harder to do things. They can't exactly *force* people."

"But I can't believe most of our friends are that nasty at heart," Eric protested.

"Maybe they aren't," agreed Samantha. "But none of them tried to resist the compulsions. Maybe they're more easily influenced or something. But they gave in, and you four didn't. So there are some who will be immune."

"Which will make them the first victims," Cassandra pointed out bleakly. "Those the monsters can't control, they'll destroy."

Connie glanced back over her shoulder, and then gave a gasp of shock. "Look!"

They all turned, and stopped, appalled. A thick, belching cloud of smoke was rising up into the clear sky.

"They've set the school on fire," whispered Cassie with utter conviction. "They've started . . ."

Samantha knew that her friend was right. "It's going to get worse," she added softly. "We've got to stay away from them. And we've got to figure out how to fight them."

"Easier said than done, in both cases," Eric objected. "Where can we go that they won't get to? Maybe the authorities?"

"The authorities might well be part of it by now," Samantha pointed out. "If even one cop is infected, he could order the rest of them to arrest us on fake charges. We can't trust the police."

"But what else can we do?" Marie asked. She looked ready to scream.

"Hide," Cassandra said firmly. "And try to find some way to fight these things. It's got to be possible." She thought for a minute. "The park," she decided. "We can hide there. Nobody will think of looking there, because it's where we hang out."

Samantha wasn't convinced this was the best idea, but she didn't have any other. Neither did the rest of them, so they accepted the suggestion by default. They hurried there, staying close together. Sammy's heart was beating fast, and not just from the exertion. At one point, they heard a siren going past, and for a second thought they were going to be spotted.

But whatever it was seemed to be traveling parallel to them, and didn't come close. Maybe it was an innocent party, but Samantha somehow doubted it.

By the time they reached the park, the cloud of smoke had become almost a wall. Thick, dark fumes were writhing into the sky, forming an overcast.

"What's happening?" Connie gasped.

"It's spreading," Cassandra answered, her face pained. "The things are gaining strength and more people are going over. They're starting new fires. And . . ." She shook her head. "I can see it," she said. "Come here, touch me. I'll see if I can share it with you."

They all moved closed, huddling together for comfort as well as contact. Samantha pressed her arms against Cassie's shoulder. As she did, a sort of unfocused picture began to form in her mind. She closed her eyes, concentrating hard on making it come clear.

After a moment, it did. It was as if she was looking out through somebody else's eyes, and what she saw appalled her. There was a mob of people, all armed with whatever weapons they could find. Some had knives; most had makeshift clubs of chair or table legs. Some had burning torches, which they were using to set fire to anything flammable. As "she" watched, one student smashed in the windows of a parked car. There was no sound, just the pictures, but Samantha winced. Another boy tore off the gas cap, and thrust a rag into the exposed gas tank. One girl with a torch lit the rag, which flared into life. Howling soundlessly, the mob ran on.

The car exploded, great gouts of flame hurtling in all directions. Several set grass and trees on fire. The students, howling and laughing, ran on.

There was a body on the ground, battered and twisted almost beyond recognition. Just scraps of bloody cloth, and red-soaked blond hair, and the shape of a human being . . .

With a ferocious anger, the insane kids were attacking anything in sight. Some of them smashed in a shop front, like looters. The shoppers inside screamed as the students poured into the supermarket. They sent displays crashing, set fire to boxes, shattered fruits and vegetables. If anyone tried to stop them, they clubbed the person mercilessly to the ground. The kids kept on hitting until their victims were no more than a bloody smear.

People ran in panic—but some joined with the mob, picking up more weapons. Several people broke into the butcher's department at the back of the store, and then ran out with arms full of knives.

In the cleaning supplies aisle, the frenzied attackers shattered bottles and jars, and then set fire to the leaking materials. A wall of flame leapt up. One of the mad kids was caught in it, his body turning into a huge torch. The others simply laughed as he thrashed around in agony, dying before their uncaring eyes.

The mob moved on, leaving the building spewing smoke and flames, heading for their next target. Waves of hatred emanated from them as they ran and screamed, hacked and burned . . .

Samantha jolted back to herself, breaking the contact with Cassandra. She was shaking and sweating uncontrollably. The people she had associated with every day, the people she'd played and joked with ... they were no longer even properly human. They were just vessels, possessed by the madness induced by the *things*. They were looking only for death, destruction, and annihilation. All that had been good or kind within them once was now submerged beneath that terrible compulsion to hate and destroy.

Everything was changed, forever.

The others had broken contact too, and were avoiding looking at one another. They all had seen what Samantha had seen, felt what she had felt. The most shattered of all, of course, was Cassie. She looked pale and tired. This was affecting her worse than most, Samantha knew, because she was still blaming herself for all of this.

"It's not your fault, Cassie," Samantha insisted, stroking her friend's still-damp hair and hugging her tightly. "It isn't."

"Then whose is it?" Cassandra demanded. "Who else can I shift the blame and the guilt to?"

"It was a combination of things," Sammy said. "Your inner talent, which you couldn't have known about. That machine of Dr. Reese's. And these *things*. They were there all along. Sooner or later, they would have discovered us anyway. It was just a matter of time."

"But I was the one who did it," Cassandra said, her voice filled with self-loathing. "All of this is my fault, no matter what you say. And I have to find a way to stop it. I *have* to! But I just don't know how."

She broke down, sobbing. Sammy cuddled her, trying desperately to protect her from everything. Especially her own guilt.

She knew that it wasn't really her friend's fault. But there was no way that she seemed to be able to get Cassie to understand this. She didn't know what she could do. Neither did Marie, Connie, Scott, or Eric. They were all lost in their own private hells, contemplating what they had all seen through Cassandra's sight.

Hell on Earth . . .

There was a loud explosion, and they all whirled around to stare back at the sight behind them. Another fire had broken out, a really large one this time. Flames had shot hundreds of feet into the air, a rippling fireball spreading death and destruction.

"A gas station," Cassandra gasped, between her tears. "They set a gas station on fire. The town won't be able to survive this. It won't."

Samantha watched as the smoke billowed out. There was so much of it now, the sky was darkening. It was as if night were falling in midafternoon. Stollville was coming to an end . . . along with most of the people she had ever known.

CHAPTER 8

CASSANDRA HAD NEVER felt so tired in her life. It was as if her new psychic abilities were draining the strength out of her, leaving her as weak as a sponge. She wanted to collapse and sleep for a week. But she couldn't do it. As strong as the *things* were now growing, as many minds as they were now possessing and controlling, that number could be doubled or tripled while she slept.

Besides, if she closed her eyes, *they* would be waiting for her, in all of their horror. Terrible, unhuman things, their raw emotions burning into her mind and soul, their hatred searing her. She couldn't face the thought of seeing them again, to be examined and despised and condemned to utter destruction.

Why those creatures should be like this, she had

no real idea. Some form of species prejudice, perhaps? Did they consider all other races as inferior vermin to be wiped out of existence? Or did they reserve some special hatred for the human race for some reason?

It hardly mattered. Whatever their motives, they were grimly determined to wipe out the human species. And she was just as determined not to allow this to happen. The major problem there was that *they* knew how to achieve their end; she didn't have the vaguest idea how to reach her own goal.

Cassandra knew that somehow she was the key. But she didn't know how to make use of this fact. She had opened the way, accidentally, for the things to get here; she alone could close it off again. But—how?

If only she wasn't so tired! If only she could think straight! If only these crashing waves of hatred didn't keep battering her! If only she could sleep . . .

Cassandra caught herself, and jerked back upright again. She had almost succumbed. Part of it was sheer tiredness, of course, but part of it was the creatures affecting her mind. They could be very subtle, making their own desires seem to be her own. That was how they had managed to take over so many people already, merging their own thoughts with those of the humans. Just a little push here, a little suggestion there—and their human victims became their willing, foolish tools. But how could it be so easy for them to turn supposedly civilized people into murdering maniacs? Everybody seemed to be affected.

Except for the few people now with her. They had managed to resist somehow. They hadn't given in to the fear and hatred and lust for destruction and death. It was possible to block out the negative, because they had managed it. But they didn't really understand how this was possible, so they couldn't make use of it.

But now she knew what the visions she'd been having were; she had somehow sensed that this was coming. *This* was what she had been seeing. The visions had been warnings, ones that she had been too stupid to understand.

Samantha laid a hand on Cassie's shoulder. "How is it?" she asked sympathetically.

"Worse," Cassandra admitted. "Much worse. I see . . ." She focused on receiving some of the random images that were bombarding her, trying to get a snatch here, a view there.

Stollville was burning. Houses, stores, gardens were all going up in flames. She saw a fire truck attempting to fight one blaze. The dedicated firemen labored to get their hoses into position to spray the flames. A crowd, howling insanely, plowed into the struggling men. Using their own weapons or snatching axes from the firemen themselves, the mob hacked the poor men to death, and then threw their bodies into the fire. They then set fire to the truck itself, laughing gleefully as the gas tank caught and exploded. They were still shrieking when the fireball engulfed them too.

Some people managed to fight off the inhuman

influence, that was obvious. The problem was that they were totally out of their depth. Anyone acting sanely or reacting with shock at what was being done was immediately targeted as an outsider—and outsiders were meant only to be destroyed. Children attacked their parents, parents their young. Old folks went down under hails of hate-filled blows. Babies were murdered. Animals, howling, barking, yowling, screeching, fled as best they could. Apparently they were beneath the notice of the *things*. Still, some of them fell victim to the random acts of violence anyway.

Cassandra's heart was near breaking at all of the death and destruction that was surrounding them as night came closer. All of those lives lost, all of those people injured and then killed. The whole town being consumed by the fires and the hatred. It was too much for her to bear. And she had started it all. She should do the world a favor and kill herself. She had intended to, until that fool Samantha had stopped her from doing the only right thing. She didn't deserve to live! After loosing this horror on the world, she should atone by killing herself too.

No! Cassandra gave a strangled cry as she realized what was happening. The creatures were attacking her again, trying to make her suicidal. True, she was guilty, but at the same time, she was the only hope that the human race now had. If she killed herself, there would be nothing left to stop the *things*.

Oh, right! As if *she* was that important! She was just having delusions of grandeur. She was nothing in the cosmic scheme of things. Just some over-evolved worm with a desire for godhood. What a fool she was to believe that!

NO!!! That wasn't the voice of reason—that was their insidious message of despair and hatred! She couldn't afford to listen to such doubts. She had to be sure of herself; she had to be strong.

She had to sleep . . .

Her body felt leaden, her blood sluggish. Her mind was shutting down bit by bit, until she would go out like a candle in the wind. She had to close her eyes, rest for a while, recover her strength. Then she'd know the answers. Then she'd be able to go on. Just a little sleep . . .

"Sammy!" she gasped, choking on her own emotions. "Help me!"

Samantha was there in a second, holding her arms. "Cassie! What is it?"

"They're attacking me, Sammy," Cassandra whispered. "Putting thoughts into my head. Trying to make me kill myself. Trying to make me give up. Trying to make me sleep." She sobbed, all of her strength gone. "Don't let them get to me, Sammy," she begged. "Keep me awake. Keep me from killing myself! Watch me, please!"

"You know I will," Samantha promised, hugging her tightly. "I won't let them get you, Cassie. I won't!"

Something was refreshing Cassandra. She could feel warmth creeping back into her chilled bones, and life into her frozen brain. There was hope again, and joy . . .

"Sammy," she said, "you're doing it! It's what I needed. I'm absorbing emotions from people, and there's so much hatred and despair right now. It's crippling me. I need your belief in me and love for me to help me hold on!"

"We can help too," Scott said, moving closer. "We believe in you, Cassie. We want you well. We want you whole." Eric, Connie, and Marie joined him.

Their emotions were real and strengthening. They were so much closer and purer than the loathing, and they were blocking it out. It was as if the lethargy and despair were being washed out of her bloodstream, and fresh, lively energy replacing it. Cassie could feel the tiredness sloughing off and her reserves being restored. Not completely—the weariness was only being held back, not vanquished. But it was a help.

And it gave her an idea.

"Positive emotions," she said excitedly. "Those creatures can only *hate*. They work with horror and despair and destruction. They don't have a handle on the good things like love and peace and joy. That's how you're all managing to drive the possession away. You won't give in to the negative, and you're concentrating on the positive."

Samantha's face glowed. "You must be right!" she exclaimed. "It makes so much sense." Then her face fell. "But look how few we are, and how many they are."

"It's always the case," Cassandra answered. "It's always easier for people to give in to evil than to strive for good. It always has been. But that has to change somehow. Anyway, I think I now know what we have to do. It's dangerous, but we don't have much choice."

Samantha glanced up at the pall of smoke in the sky. They could all see and hear the fires crackling through what was left of their homes. The air was laden with ashes, the stench of burning gas and charred flesh. Cassandra didn't want to even start thinking about where that stench was coming from. "So, right now *anything* is dangerous," she said softly. "What do we have to do?"

"We have to find everyone who has managed to escape being possessed," Cassie said, conviction filling her as she spoke. This was the right thing to do— she knew it! "Gather them together. Keep one another safe. And then we'll all meet up. If the four of you can give me enough positive energy to keep me going, then imagine what twenty or thirty might do for me. I'm picturing a sort of emotional laser beam. If we can fire nothing but positive emotions at the *things,* that should send them reeling. They wouldn't be able to handle that. It might even be sufficient to seal the gateway, cutting them off from us again. At the very least, it will shock and scare them."

Connie looked worried. "You want us to go out there? Cassie, we'll all get *killed!*"

"It's possible, yes," Cassandra agreed, her heart heavy again. "Like I said, it's very dangerous. But we can't stay here, anyway. They're bound to attack the park sooner or later, and if we stay here we're likely to be trapped."

"True enough," agreed Scott. He nodded. "Okay.

We'll have to chance it. Anyway, if we find enough people who believe us, then we can fight back."

"No!" Cassie said, scared. "You mustn't even *think* about fighting! That's a negative emotion, and the entities might be able to use that to get at you! They might make you attack the possessed. No, you've got to focus only on helping and saving people. Bringing them together for good. Don't allow any negative thoughts inside, or it will all be corrupted and turned against you."

Scott bowed his head, ashamed. "I'm sorry, Cassie. I wasn't thinking."

"You're doing very well," she said. Bending forward, she kissed his cheek. She could feel the warmth of his emotions at that, like a fire of its own, warming her soul. Maybe she should try kissing a few more people! That was a very positive emotion, and would certainly help her out.

Later . . .

"Right," she said. "We'd better split up. We'll cover more ground this way. We'll all meet up as soon as we can. Where?" She racked her brains, trying to think of a good spot.

"The school," Samantha suggested.

"Bless you!" Cassie exclaimed. Thank goodness for Sammy's sharp mind! "That's where they broke through first, so that's where we should fight back. And they've destroyed it, so they wouldn't think of searching for us there, would they? We'll all meet at the school as soon as we can. Then we'll link together, and I'll try to focus all of the good and pure thoughts we can at these monsters. It will work, I know it will! I've touched their minds and souls so much already, and they always make me shudder at what there is in there. There's no goodness of any kind. Pure, decent emotions will at least shock them, and with luck it will seal them off from us forever." She felt totally renewed at this hope.

"Right," Samantha agreed. "We can do it. I know we can!"

The other four mumbled their agreement. Cassie could feel their reluctance and fear. But they all understood that this was their only chance now.

"Besides," Eric added, "it's our duty. If there's anyone else left alive out there, we have to find them and help them. We can't just hide away and do nothing."

"Right," Marie agreed. "This is the only hope for all of us." She managed a wan grin for Cassie. "We'd better not all go at once, or in the same directions. We'll be more likely to get past those people if we go at different times and in different directions."

"Good thinking," Samantha agreed. "Okay, I'll head east, you head west. The rest of you wait ten minutes or so. Then Eric, you go north, and Connie, go south." She smiled at Cassie. "You just go wherever you like."

"Oh, great," Cassandra said, pretending to be upset. "Make me think for myself!" She hugged Samantha tightly. "Be careful."

"You know me," Samantha said, her voice tight with emotion. "Careful is my middle name." Cassandra could feel the strength flowing from her friend. She released Samantha, and then Scott hugged her and kissed her cheek. Once again, Cassie felt slightly renewed from this flow of positive emotion.

The two of them then left, in opposite directions. Cassandra felt their loss, as well as fear for their safety. But they had to try this. There really wasn't any other option.

"Will they be okay, do you think?" asked Connie softly.

"They've got to be," Cassandra answered, trying to believe it herself. "This is our only hope of defeating the creatures. We *have* to overload them with pure, positive energy. And anyone who isn't yet possessed is our only source."

"I know." Connie lapsed into silence, obviously worried about her own chances. Eric was similarly brooding. Cassandra understood, and didn't intrude.

She was starting to tire again when Eric sighed and moved toward her. "Time to go," he announced, sounding glum. He gave her a hug and a quick peck on the cheek. "See you later."

"Yes," Connie said, striving to sound really sure of herself, but failing rather badly. She couldn't hide her true emotions from Cassandra. But Cassie appreciated the attempt. Her hug gave Cassandra more strength. Slowly, the two of them walked away, and Cassandra was alone.

She felt this very acutely. It was as if suddenly a spotlight had been turned on her. The four of them had been helping to shield her against attack, and now she had nothing to rely upon but her own strength. Would that be enough to hold out?

It had to be! The doubts and fears were just the

images that the creatures were projecting into her mind. Well, no, that simply wasn't true. Cassie had plenty of doubts and fears of her own. But the *things* were adding to them, piling anxiety and terror upon them. Cassandra whimpered under the assault. But she refused to give in.

Slowly, she moved away from her hiding place. As she did so, she saw and felt movement in the distance. There was a roar as gasoline caught fire, and then crackling as trees began to char.

The mob had set fire to the park now!

It might simply be part of their mindless violence. But she couldn't rule out the possibility that the creatures had now been able to focus in on where she was, and were intent on driving her out and into the arms of the crowd.

Cassandra ran. The direction didn't matter, as long as it was away from the fire. Or was that the trick? Was the fire meant to drive her, just as she was running? Was there a mob waiting for her to emerge from the park? She hesitated, confused. What should she do?

Run parallel to the fire, she decided. *Try to beat it to the edge of the park.* That was the answer! She passed the duck pond, now totally bereft of life of any kind. Had the birds flown away, terrified by the noises and smells? Or had they been caught and slaughtered by the insane mob? It hardly mattered right now.

Cassandra reached the edge of the park just as the flames were growing higher. They were roaring fiercely against the sky, sending up more thick smoke. She could feel a wall of heat hammering against her bare skin. It was an inferno back there! Trees were torches, blazing high and then collapsing in showers of flames and sparks. She couldn't even hear them fall over the noise of the fire.

And then she saw the shapes of people. Some were *in* the fire, burning. But others were ahead of the flames, moving quickly, armed with anything they could find. They were howling like animals, waving their weapons. Perhaps they were just running to avoid the fire, but some were heading toward her.

If they caught her, she was dead . . .

Panicking, terrified, Cassandra fled for her life.

CHAPTER 9

SAMANTHA WAS WALKING through a nightmare. Stollville had simply ceased to exist. Nothing remained of the town where she had lived all of her life. There were still streets, and charred hunks of masonry, the stumps of trees and telephone poles and the shattered bases of street-lamps. But very little else.

A fine gray ash was consuming everything, the remnants of the burning process. The powdery, choking stuff was falling from the sky like snow, covering everything in a gentle blanket of grayness. There was the stench of woodsmoke, gasoline, and charred flesh. She didn't want to think about the source of the latter.

Was this what the world had come to? A giant conflagration fueled by hatred? Were people so easily driven to murder and destruction? It was a scary thought.

What had happened to all of the people she knew? Those she was related to? Mom and Dad might be safe, because they worked out of town. Except, of course, Samantha didn't know how widespread this was. Was it limited just to Stollville? Or was it happening all over the world right now? There was no way of telling. If it *had* spread, then no one was safe.

What about her kid brother, Tony? He would have been at school when this began. Was he part of the crowd? Or one of its victims? Or had he somehow managed to escape? She felt a fire in her heart as she thought about him. There was no way to know until this was over . . .

She realized that her cheeks were damp from tears she didn't even know she was crying. It was so wrenching in her soul to be so unsure. Almost everyone that she loved could be dead or else possessed by now.

No! They were negative thoughts, leaving her open to attack by those creatures! She couldn't allow herself to be distracted by thoughts of her family now.

And what about her other friends? Ashley was dead already, and Troy had been jailed. But the mob must have attacked the jail. Where was Troy now? Part of the mob? He'd been the first victim of possession, after all. How many of her friends were now screaming for blood, or had their hands covered in it? Even if somehow Cassie managed to stop this thing, how could anyone go back to normal after what had been done? If someone had killed and burned and destroyed, and they were made whole again—how could they possibly live with the knowledge of what they had done?

It was those aliens again, nagging at her with distracting, terrible thoughts! She had to fight them, and not give in to them. There had to be a way out of this, and Cassie would find it. Samantha simply had to have faith in her friend, that was all. And ignore the terrible, whispering thoughts and gut-wrenching feelings.

Samantha moved through the destroyed streets. She heard the sound of a motor a short distance away, and then a crashing sound. She didn't know what it meant at first, until she realized that somebody must have found construction equipment and was using it to demolish houses and stores. The mob was determined to obliterate everything that mankind had made.

She stumbled over something half-hidden in the ashes. She almost threw up when she saw that it was a corpse, bloody and battered. So many deaths already . . . and more to come, no doubt. Was there even anyone left alive and untouched by the madness? And if so, how could she possibly find them?

Well, they'd be hiding out or trying to flee the mob, that was obvious. She'd have to stay away from the focus of destruction to find anyone. Besides, she realized, she had a little something extra that might just help: her psychic ability. She might not be as good as Cassie, but if she could call fifty-two cards right every time, she should be able to locate a living person, right? Of course, calling cards was one thing and finding people another . . .

She took a deep breath, and then regretted it. Coughing, she realized that all of the ash and stench was fighting against her, too. It was hard to concentrate in this kind of atmosphere. Well, there wasn't another right now, so she'd just have to put up with it. She took shallower breaths, which helped. Maybe what she really needed was a wet handkerchief over her nose and mouth. That was supposed to help. But she had neither a handkerchief—she had no idea what had happened to her bag—nor a source of water, anyway.

The thought of water made her realize just how thirsty she was. And hungry. How long had it been since she'd last taken a bite, or a sip? She honestly couldn't remember. Her stomach growled, and her throat was parched.

No! It was those creatures again! Now they were trying to prey on her discomfort. There were more important things to think about now than her empty stomach and dry throat. Like staying alive. And beating those things.

Samantha forced herself to ignore her discomfort and to focus instead on finding survivors. There had to be more out there, somewhere. If she could just somehow use her powers . . . but she didn't know how! What was the point of trying to use her abilities if she didn't have a clue as to how they worked?

Stop it! she screamed at herself. That was the aliens thinking at her again. It didn't matter *how* she did it but simply that it worked. She cleared her mind of doubts and fears, forcing herself to focus only on good thoughts, good people.

And then she *knew*. There was someone not too far away, hiding, shivering. Samantha could feel the fear, as strong as if a light were shining in her face. With confidence, she followed this feeling. She had to watch her footing and listen for signs of pursuit. But it sounded like the crazies were heading away from her, at least for now.

A couple of streets later, she saw the battered wreckage of a house. Fires still burned in the ruins spasmodically, but there wasn't much left to consume. The house had been burned to the ground, and the walls and roof had collapsed downward. Yet her instincts told her that there was somebody alive here. How could anyone have survived this? Samantha moved forward, losing confidence in her feeling. Yet it insisted that someone was indeed here . . .

She stepped onto the warm wreckage, probing about, trying to narrow down the life signs with her mind. Somewhere . . . downward . . . She saw a storm door for a cellar, half burned, and then realized that this was where the survivor had to be. She moved to it, pushing aside the smoldering wood. Steps led down into darkness. She walked slowly down, and the feeling of life grew stronger.

Somebody whimpered, and the sound was cut off.

"Hello," Samantha called quietly. She didn't want to be heard outside of this cellar. "It's all right, I'm not going to hurt you. I'm still normal."

No reply. Whoever was here must be terrified that this was a trick.

"Please believe me," Samantha said, moving through the darkness, feeling her way cautiously so she wouldn't bark her shins or fall over anything. "I'm trying to find survivors, to bring us together. I'm telling the truth." She tried to use her mind to project sincerity, hoping that it would somehow get through to whomever was here.

A moment later, she heard a movement, and then a terrified, quiet voice: "I'm here. Please God, are you *really* okay?" It sounded like an old lady.

"Yes," Samantha said, feeling elated. There *were* others still alive! "I'm so glad I've found you!"

There was a slight movement, and then she could barely make out a shape in the blackness. It moved toward her, and she grasped at it, hugging. There was a muffled cry, and Samantha realized that the old lady was carrying something.

"My grandson," the woman gasped. "He's scared and hungry, and I was so afraid he'd make noise and draw them to me. The world's gone mad!"

"Yes, it has," Samantha agreed. "We've got to get out of here, though."

"It's not safe up there!" the old woman gasped. "They're killing people and burning everything! I thought we'd die when they set my house on fire. But the cellar stayed intact. We've been hiding in the darkness for hours."

"I know it's not safe," Samantha agreed. "But we're trying to get all of the survivors together at the high school. Once we're there, we think we can stop the powers that are causing this terrible disaster." She explained briefly what was happening. "I know it's hard to believe," she summed up. "But it's our only chance. If we don't do this, nothing will stop those creatures until they've wiped out all the human race."

"It does sound far-fetched," the woman agreed. "But . . . well, so does what has happened. It's like the end of the world."

"Yes," Sammy said. "It might even come to that. We don't know. But we have to fight back. We can't let these monsters just do it."

"No," said the old lady. "All right, I'll come with you. Is there anyone else alive, aside from your friends?"

Samantha concentrated, trying to reach out and touch another person. "Yes," she said with conviction. "I can tell there's somebody about a quarter of a mile away. Let's go. And you *have* to keep the baby quiet. I can't tell where the enemy are, and if they hear anything, they'll kill us."

"Of course."

Together, they left the cellar. The old lady gave a gasp of shock as she saw the world about her. "It's so desolate," she whispered. She was disheveled, and her hair was a mess. There was a dirt stain down one cheek. She clutched her grandson to her feverishly. Samantha hoped she wasn't going to suffocate him.

"It doesn't get better," Samantha said apologetically. "Come on, this way."

They worked their way to another wrecked house. In this case, the person hiding was a young boy. He'd slipped into a drainage pipe near the end of his bleak garden, and was shaking in there when they found him. He couldn't have been more than four years old. The old lady hugged him to her skirts, and he stuck to her side like a limpet.

Samantha worked on as the day waned. Or was it night? The sky was completely overcast, cutting off all indications of time. If it weren't for the glow from the fires, the whole town would be dark. As it was, the light was pretty weak. They were constantly stumbling, either over wreckage or bodies. Samantha was shocked at how indifferent she was growing toward seeing corpses. At the start, she'd wanted to vomit; now she was hardly sparing them a second glance. Well, she supposed you could get used to anything if you saw it often enough. What a terrible thought!

One by one, she managed to gather survivors. Two mothers with babies; four young men; a supermarket clerk who'd survived inside a freezer and had been in danger of dying of asphyxiation when they'd broken down the door to release her. Three couples. Most had hidden in cellars, or in the ruins. Some had been scared to trust Samantha, but eventually all of them had joined her.

It was time, she realized, though she didn't know how she'd come to that awareness. "We have to go to the school now," she said gently. They'd managed to avoid the marauding gangs so far, but there was no sense in taking undue risks. "We'll join the others there. Then we'll see about striking back. As soon as Cassie gets there, we can fight again."

Samantha hoped she could find her way back to the school. It was hard telling where they were. The street signs were all gone, and everywhere looked pretty much like everywhere else in this desolation. But, once again, her psychic sense came to the rescue. One way just seemed *right,* and so she led the group in that direction. Stumbling, tired, and dispirited, the rest of them followed her. Nobody disputed her right to lead them.

The scenery never improved. Ash lay over everything, as if this was some modern-day Pompeii, ravaged by an exploding volcano. Stubs of buildings poked up through the grayness. Clouds of smoke hovered. Small fires snapped and burned. Embers glowed. It was heartbreaking, slouching through the ruins. The group followed her like zombies, their spirits too battered to protest.

Finally, they made it to what had once been the school. Now there was barely anything to suggest it had been a proud building only hours earlier. Rubble and twisted metal poked out of the inevitable ash. The playing fields were scorched earth. The trees were shattered matches. There was a hole in the ground, blackened and stinking, where the oil tank that powered the heating system had once been. It must have exploded early on. The wreckage was still warm, but not uncomfortably so.

Some of the walls were still upright to about eight feet, though not many. "We can hide in here," Samantha decided. "Go ahead. Post a lookout so you'll know if the mob comes back. I'm going to stay here and wait for the others to arrive."

"How will we know that they're normal?" asked one of the survivors.

"If they aren't screaming, burning, and killing, they're with us," Samantha answered. "There will be more, I'm sure of it." She couldn't explain how she could possibly know this, but she did.

The others accepted what she said, and moved to hide in the ruins. One of the couples appointed themselves sentries, and they stayed on the fringe, hugging each other tightly for whatever comfort they could give one another. It had to be small enough, considering their situation.

Samantha looked out into the bleakness, wondering where the others were. She could feel in her mind their approach. Each of them had managed to find a few other people, but it was a pitifully small remnant of a whole town.

Scott arrived first, with seven others. They all looked as shocked and tired as the ones she'd rescued. Samantha guided them to hide with her group. Scott gave her a bear hug. "I'm so glad you're okay," he murmured. "I really thought that the gang would get us all. But we avoided them. I can't imagine how."

Samantha had been trying to avoid thinking about it, but she knew she couldn't deny the obvious any longer. "It's Cassie," she explained, her emotions numb. "She's been their target all along. They've been hunting for her, and leaving us alone. That's the only reason we made it."

"Makes sense," he agreed grimly. "Then the others are probably okay, too."

"They're on their way," Samantha promised him. She stared out into the darkness. "In fact, here's one of them now."

It was Connie, with eight people. Then Eric arrived with six. Finally, Marie staggered in, looking totally exhausted, with another seven.

"It's not many," she said wearily. "But it's all we could manage. There're so few of us left."

"But more than before," Samantha said, trying to be upbeat about it. "That's over fifty of us. When Cassie gets here, we should be more than enough to help her to break through." The newcomers were all moving to join the others. Nobody could move quickly, and most seemed to be broken people. Samantha couldn't blame them, considering what they had all been through.

Scott shifted uneasily. He, Eric, Connie, and Marie had stayed with her, crouched in the ruins, surveying the night. "What about Cassie?" he asked, afraid of her reply. "Is she okay? Can she get to us?"

"She's hurting badly," Samantha said, able to reach out to her friend. "She's so tired and shaken. But she's managing to come here. The savages are hunting her, though. Still, once she's here, it won't matter. I know that there will be enough of us here to help her. We *can* end it. I'm certain of that."

Connie gave a gasp, and pointed. "I saw somebody moving out there. Is it another survivor?"

Samantha surveyed the area. "No," she said coldly. "I can't feel anybody real out there. It has to be somebody from the mob. They may have been looking for us." They all went silent, hugging the warm rubble beneath their stomachs for protection. Sammy saw a movement, and then a second, and a third . . .

"They know we're here," she breathed, realizing the truth. "They *let* us gather everybody together."

Marie choked. "They wanted to get us into one place. All the normal people who were left. They wanted us together so that they could kill us."

That was it exactly. Samantha scanned the darkness, and saw that the mob was closing in . . . for the kill.

CHAPTER 10

CASSANDRA STOOD IN the nothingness, confused. Where was she? What was she doing here? How long had she been here? She had no answers to any of these questions. Only a deep-seated weariness within her soul. She didn't know very much at all. Even recollecting her name was almost impossible. She was just so exhausted, it was hard to stay awake. Yet she knew that she *must* stay awake. And that there was something very important that she had to do.

If only she could remember what it was.

Meeting. Meet someone. Meet . . . That was it. Somehow, somewhere, she was supposed to meet someone.

She glanced out into the darkness. She could *feel*

the people out there, the sick, twisted minds that wanted to find her and rip her to tiny little pieces and then dance in savage joy on every bloody fragment. None of those were the people she was supposed to meet. She was sure of that. They were looking for her, and she was avoiding them.

Cassandra staggered on, kicking up fine dust, coughing, but trying to stay as silent as possible. Whom, then, was she supposed to meet? If only she weren't so tired, her mind so drained. If only she could stop a while and slumber. But even though she couldn't remember why, she knew that sleep would be the worst possible thing.

Was there anyone normal left in the world? She didn't know. All she could do was open her mind to the possibility.

And *something* responded. Something alive, and scared, and in need.

There was someone else around, then! The thought gave her comfort and strength. She shuffled off toward the warmth she could sense in her mind, knowing this was the right thing to do. Maybe she was touching Sammy . . .

Sammy! Now she could remember! Her best friend, Samantha. That's who she had to meet! She laughed, but quietly, not wishing to draw attention to herself. It was starting to come back to her, little by little, as she focused. Maybe soon she'd remember where Sammy was.

The life force drew her, and she was puzzled. It didn't seem quite right somehow. But she didn't know why. Maybe the person was injured? Was that it? She couldn't tell, only that it was around here somewhere . . .

Here being a burned-out shell of a house, almost leveled to the ground. She looked around. The life source was there, in the corner, under shattered bricks. She reached it, and called out quietly: "I'm here. I'll help. Don't worry." The life below heard and seemed to understand. There was a longing for help and company.

Her nails were broken already, so she didn't care that they were chipped as she dug through the bricks. Below the bricks was the wreckage of some sort of bookcase, it seemed. It had fallen down on something, and wasn't quite resting on the floor. Then the wall had collapsed onto it, forming a sort of cave below. Cassie pulled bricks away, and then felt excitement as the survivor must have seen her.

Something wet stroked her hand.

Confused, she paused, and then pulled out the last of the bricks blocking the way. There was a tiny whine, and a small dog crawled out of the wreckage. It was barely more than a puppy, she realized. Some sort of terrier, all black. It licked her hand gratefully again.

A *dog?* She'd rescued a dog? She'd been hoping for another person, and she got a puppy? She felt terribly disappointed, and then the dog clambered to her, whining, seeking comfort.

"Poor boy," she murmured, feeling sorry for him. She picked him up and cradled him in her arms. "It must have been terrifying for you. But it's okay now." She could feel trust and relief radiating from it. And somehow that made her stronger, more able to concentrate. Right. She was some sort of emotional sponge. She had powers that enabled her to draw on the emotions of others.

To fight the *things* in the nightmare world!

Her memory flooded back to her now. Cassie recalled all that had happened. The positive emotions flowing from the puppy were strong enough to revitalize her! Now she remembered Sammy and the meeting at the school.

It was time that she was there!

Cassandra had recovered some of her strength. Clutching the puppy to her chest like a baby, she hurried through the ruins in the direction of the school. Now she was more alert, and she could make sense of what was happening. After Sammy and the rest had left her, the *things* had focused in on her. Unable to draw emotional strength from the others, Cassie had been an easy target for the hatred. She'd been dazed and damaged, barely able to think. Now, however, she was getting stronger. All thanks to this puppy! She hugged it happily, and it licked her filthy cheek.

The mob had been hunting her, striving to kill her. But she had retained enough strength to hide from them. So where were they?

The puppy whined, disturbed. Then Cassie smelled blood in the air. Shock and horror gripped her heart; had the mob caught and killed her friends? Dear God, please not!

Cassandra saw shapes in the road ahead. She was

terrified to look, but knew that she had no choice. Slowly, she walked to the closest, afraid it would be Marie, or Connie, or—worst of all—Sammy. She forced herself to look down on the still-bleeding body. It was very fresh, killed only a half hour or less ago, she realized. And it was some girl from school she vaguely knew.

The weird thing was that she had a knife still clutched in her left hand. There was drying blood on it. She was one of the mad ones. Who could have killed her?

And then Cassie knew, shuddering at the thought. They were turning on each other now. That was the way *they* would want it, of course. Once the sane were dead, then the possessed would kill one another, and there would be no life left on the Earth at all.

Did that mean that Sammy and the rest were already dead? That there were no more victims for the insane? No, she refused to believe that! It was more likely that they had turned on one another because they simply couldn't find any other victims. It meant that Samantha and the rest had managed to stay hidden. It *had* to mean that!

Stepping carefully to avoid the pools of congealing blood, Cassie hurried on toward the school. It was coming to a head now, she knew. The showdown. She had to be there to gather what strength, love, and encouragement she could from the survivors.

Not far now. She didn't recognize any of the streets, of course. It was all rubble and ashes. But she knew instinctively that this was the right way.

Ahead, she could just about feel the strength of Sammy and the rest. But there was something odd about it that she couldn't place, and it worried her.

Finally, the ruins of the school came into sight. And her heart sank.

Gathered all around the last vestiges of the walls and rooms were the people of the mob. They had surrounded the survivors, a ring of weapons, ready to kill. Cassandra winced as she realized that her plan had actually played into the monsters' hands. By gathering the sane together, she'd provided the insane with their final targets in one convenient place.

"No," she whispered, refusing to accept that this was the end of her plan. All she had to do was to get through this circle and join with her friends.

As one, the crowd turned to stare in her direction. They *knew* she was here. And they would never let her pass! Cassandra tried to link with Sammy and the rest. She felt a faint stirring, but not enough. She was still too far away.

"You won't get closer." Cassie stared at the speaker, and then realized that it was Troy. His face was twisted; his bare arms leaked blood. He held an antique sword in his hand, and in his eyes there was only madness. "We know who you are, Cassie," he said, his voice tinged with madness. "We know your plan. And it might have worked, too. Only it won't, because you can never get through us to join your friends in there." He laughed madly. "And they won't get out to you. Just to us, and they won't survive that."

"Troy," Cassie begged, "there must be something of you left in there! You can't let those things do this! They'll destroy everything worthwhile. You have to fight them! Help me!"

"Sorry, sweetie," Troy laughed. "It's too late for that. Far, far too late. All you can do is give in and die."

"No!" Cassandra yelled. "I won't! That's what *they* want, and I won't do it!"

Troy raised the sword, grinning. "You don't understand, do you? You don't know who the monsters are yet! Go on, try to reach them now. See what you get." He laughed. "I can wait."

Cassie didn't understand what he was talking about. But contacting the watchers, the things that haunted the darkness, was just what she wanted. Why was he so keen for her to do it? She didn't know, but she had to seize her chance. She focused on the *things*.

And they were *here*, surrounding her. She could feel them, feel their loathing. They weren't in the shadows any longer, and, at last, she could make them out.

Cassie gasped in shock.

They weren't alien creatures at all. They were twisted, malformed human figures. They were Troy and Paula and other people she had thought she knew. But their faces, their hearts, they were all wrong, warped out of true . . .

Staring at Troy, Cassie finally understood. There were no watchers. There were no aliens. That had just been how her mind had tried to cope with what she had been sensing. She had thought they were aliens because they seemed to be so inhuman. And they hated goodness. But what they were instead was the shadow inside all people—the brute, the primitive, the part that hated goodness and light. The part that wanted to be free, to live in the daylight, to be in control, instead of being repressed behind the positive emotions that managed to keep the hatred and the horror in check.

The monsters were the dark recesses of the human soul.

They were within, not without . . .

The puppy whined in Cassie's arms, and she hugged it protectively. "I won't let him hurt you," she whispered. "I promise." The puppy seemed content with her impossible vow, and licked her cheek again. Strength filled her.

And then she knew what to do.

She closed her eyes. Troy and the others were watching her reactions and enjoying it. They were waiting for the final curtain to fall on the few people left with decency and hope. And then the earth would belong to them.

You can't have them, she thought at the things. *I won't let you.*

You can't stop us, the voice of the many told her. They stood, facing her and despising her for what she was. And, under it all, there was a fear that she somehow might still be able to stop them. *Using positive emotions was the right way. But you're not strong enough by yourself. And you cannot reach your friends.*

"I don't need to!" Cassie cried, praying that she was right. "You're so contemptuous of all other life forms, aren't you? You don't understand anything at all!" She bent to rub her cheek to the dog. "Humans aren't the only creatures capable of positive emotions."

She focused on the puppy. She felt its trust in her, its affection and gratitude. It had been lost and hurt and frightened. And then she had found it, and held it, and loved it.

It loved her back, simply and unconditionally, and it trusted her with its life, without reservation. The love and trust that only a dog can give.

And then she sent this out at the things with all the intensity that she could manage.

NOOOOOOOOOOO . . .

The scream echoed inside her head and soul. The overwhelming power of the projection slammed into the once-human creatures. Their shriveled, evil souls couldn't take it. It was like daylight breaking on the shores of night, shattering the darkness and bringing day. The tortured, twisted beings screamed in agony as the power of simple love and trust crashed into them.

They had given in to the darkness within their own souls, and had destroyed the good that had been within them. Troy had killed Ashley because he had loved her. The only way he could destroy his love was to destroy the object of his love. That action had freed his inner being, the horror that now possessed him. The others, too, had killed all that they had any affection for, and there was nothing good left within themselves. Only evil. They couldn't stand up against goodness now; they had no defense against it. It burned their mental processes; it fried their souls.

They burned, cold and sharp, like moths in a flame. Single bursts of energy, snapping up and out, dying and vanishing into nothingness. One by one they howled and flamed and died.

Cassandra opened her eyes to take in the scene before her.

Troy had almost reached her with the sword when he had started to die. He had frozen in place, his mad eyes bulging, his face twisted into a sneer, his muscles spasming. Then his legs gave way, and he collapsed forward, pitching down into the ash, stiff and lifeless.

One by one, all of the other zombies did the same. There was nothing of their human selves left any longer, and without the driving force of the inner evil, there was nothing keeping them together. In a wave, all of the insane crashed to the ground, finally dead.

For several moments, nothing happened. But there was a curious sensation of peace inside Cassie's mind. The link with the darkness was gone, severed by the flames that had burned the twisted maniacs. She was free of that nightmare at last.

There was movement again, and Cassie stirred. A momentary alarm made her wonder if the mad ones were not dead, but reviving. And then she realized that it was the survivors, venturing out of their hiding places. One of them ran, haltingly, toward Cassie. She realized that it was Sammy—battered, bloody, but unswayed. She laughed as she ran, and then she grabbed and hugged Cassie.

"You did it," she whispered. "You drove them off! They're gone!"

"Yes," Cassie agreed. She hugged her friend back, until the puppy protested. "They're gone, finally. And we're free." She stared at the small group of people who were dazedly emerging from the ruins. A pitifully small number. "Is this it?"

Samantha nodded, her mood turning solemn. "It's all we could find," she admitted. "So very few . . . but we're alive and together."

"Yes." Cassie knew she was too weary to be able to react properly. So few left . . . What about her mom? Everyone else she knew? Were they among the dead? Or had they somehow managed to survive elsewhere? And what was she going to tell these survivors? That the monsters had been only what was left of their friends? That there were no aliens? That Troy and the others had been responsible for their own terrible evil? Or should she keep this foul truth to herself?

"Now what do we do?" That was Scott, as he, Eric, Marie, and Connie reached her. "They're gone. What do we do?"

Cassie hadn't even considered that. "We can't stay here," she said slowly. "There isn't anything left. And we need food, and water, and, above all, rest. We won't get it here."

"Can we get it anywhere?" Connie asked, wiping her hair back from her eyes. "Is there anywhere that is undamaged?"

"I don't know." Cassie didn't have the strength left to try to see with her mind. Maybe later. "I don't even know how widespread this was. It might have only seized our town. Or it might have gripped the whole world. Or something in between. I don't know."

"If it was just our town," Sammy pointed out, "surely someone would have been investigating by now? Planes, or cars, or that sort of thing."

"Maybe they tried," Eric said. "But they wouldn't have managed to get through. Not while the *things* had control." He looked up at the sky. "Maybe they can get through now, though."

"If there is anyone else." Cassie wished she could be more positive, but she couldn't. She was too numb. "Meanwhile, we *will* survive. We have to get out of here. We need to find something untouched. Come on."

Slowly, she turned her back on the death and destruction. Her tired feet began to move, leading the way out of the ruins of Stollville. Hopefully there would be something left alive outside of the town.

Hopefully.

At least hope was a positive emotion. And they still had those.

Sammy walked beside her, which felt good. And Cassie cradled in her arms the puppy that had helped to save the world. Whatever was left of it.

They would survive. Cassie would make certain of that.

Epilogue

SOMETIMES A DREAM is just a dream—
fleeting images that fade when you
waken. But at other times, the dreams are only a
shadow of what is to come. A way to break through
the limitations of time and space.

And who knows what mankind will find when it
ventures beyond the limits that it already knows?
What things there are, and what minds they might
have?

Or what price such knowledge may demand?

THIS STORY IS OVER.

BUT YOUR JOURNEY INTO

THE OUTER LIMITS™

HAS ONLY BEGUN....

TOR BOOKS

 Check out these titles from
Award-Winning Young Adult Author
NEAL SHUSTERMAN

Enter a world where reality takes a U-turn...

MindQuakes: Stories to Shatter Your Brain

"A promising kickoff to the series. Shusterman's mastery of suspense and satirical wit make the ludicrous fathomable and entice readers into suspending their disbelief. He repeatedly interjects plausible and even poignant moments into otherwise bizzare scenarios...[T]his all-too-brief anthology will snare even the most reluctant readers."—*Publishers Weekly*

MindStorms: Stories to Blow Your Mind

MindTwisters: Stories that Play with Your Head

And don't miss these exciting stories from Neal Shusterman:

Scorpion Shards
"A spellbinder."—*Publishers Weekly*

"Readers [will] wish for a sequel to tell more about these interesting and unusual characters."—*School Library Journal*

The Eyes of Kid Midas
"Hypnotically readable!"—*School Library Journal*

Dissidents
"An involving read."—*Booklist*